Produced by LouLou Productions LLC

Copyright © 2012 by David Carner

Cover design by C. M. Rogers

EPUB ISBN: 978-0-9859514-0-5

Kindle ISBN: 978-0-9859514-1-2

Paperback ISBN: 978-0-9859514-2-9

To find out more about John Fowler, please feel free to follow my author page on Facebook. The David Carner fan page currently holds all announcements pertaining to this series. Also check out www.davidcarner.com for information on this series and any other works. You may also follow me on twitter @davidcarner.

The John Fowler Novels

The Road to Justice

Sins of the Son

This Thing of Our

Journey's End

Day's Past (Coming Christmas 2014)

Check out http://david-carner.blogspot.com/ for my free short story, Bad Day in Queen's Landing. The blog is updated with a new chapter weekly.

To Mom and Dad (George): Thank you for raising me to believe in myself and teaching me that I can do anything I put my mind to.

To Chelle and LouLou: Thank you. Thank you for believing in me and encouraging me at every opportunity.

To my Great-Uncle Bill (who is no longer with us): Almost 30 years ago, you gave me a collection of works by Sir Arthur Conan Doyle and introduced me to the world's greatest detective. Thank you for believing in a young boy and his love for reading.

To Bobbi: Every time I was stuck, had a question, needed advice, something proofread (I honestly believe you saw every version of every query letter I sent to agents), or just a kind word, you helped me out. I cannot thank you enough for all the help you have been.

To Tonya: Each time I was ready to quit on this project you seemed to magically know I needed encouragement. Thank you from the bottom of my heart.

To Mr. Rogers: You saved me on technicalities more than once, and for that, you have my heartfelt gratitude. Thank you.

To Mr. George: You've been my rock through this whole thing. I don't say it often, but as far as I'm concerned you and Mr. Wilhelm are the brothers I never had. Thank you.

To Mr. Wilhelm: Thank you. Fourteen years ago, you encouraged me to write fantasy wrestling. You wrote your organization and I wrote mine. You pushed me to tap into my creative side. This book would never have been possible without you. As I said to Mr. George, you're the brother I never had. Thank you.

To Lester and Rhonda: Thank you for supporting me and believing in me. I can honestly tell you without all of your support this never would have happened.

To all of those who have supported me financially: Thank you. Without your help, LouLou Productions LLC never would have formed, and there never would have been a physical copy of my work. Thank you from the bottom of my heart.

Thank you to Ahmad, Amy, Amy, Carrie, Clint, Elizabeth, Leigh Ann, Linda, Nancy, Rob, Susan, and Steve. Thank you for critiquing my work and helping me stay on track. Without all of you, this never would have happened.

Finally to you, the reader: Thank you for picking up a novel from an unknown author and giving me a chance. I hope you enjoy the story I am about to share with you.

Chapter 1

Sunlight streamed into the apartment window as John continued to beat on his alarm clock. As the buzzing continued, John realized it was his phone and not the alarm clock making the horrible racket. As he focused his eyes on the name flashing on his phone, John groaned. "Mommy" continued to flash across the face of his phone as John set his feet on the floor and held his head in his hands. It wasn't his real Mother, of course. His real Mother hadn't spoken to him in three years now; which was fine by him. In fact, John couldn't remember speaking to any of his family since the funeral.

"No," thought John. "They would speak to me; I just don't want to speak to them . . . not since I made that scene at the gravesite after the funeral."

The funeral; it had been three years, and it still seemed like yesterday. It seemed like just yesterday when his father-in-law cussed him in front of everyone at the gravesite. It probably didn't help that John was three sheets to the wind while his father-in-law was doing it. It probably didn't help that John had told Arthur, John's father-in-law, that he was an interfering waste of human flesh. It probably didn't help that he told Arthur that John and Sam had never had children, not because of John's job, but because Sam didn't want Arthur's interfering nose in the child's life. It sure didn't help that Arthur was right about John. If John hadn't been drinking. If . . . John's thoughts were interrupted by the phone buzzing again.

John stood up and stretched. He glanced out the window at the city. New York. Sam had wanted to live here. "Where else can you find the arts, the different types of people, the nightlife, and all the other wonders this city held?" she had asked him. The most exciting city in the world . . . for Sam; for John, it was the loneliest city in the

5

world. John had only one friend here. Most of John's friends apparently agreed with the words his father-in-law had spoken. In fact, except for Chet, none of his friends had spoken to him since the funeral. That was fine with John. He didn't need anyone. No sirree, he was doing just fine on his own.

"They say every cloud has a silver lining and the silver lining is that I haven't had to listen to your stupidity, Arthur, since I lost her. I don't have to listen to your judgments, your foolish ideas, and I don't have to listen to you speak." John smiled. As he glanced over to the picture on his nightstand of himself and the beautiful girl with him, his stomach dropped all over again. The smile fell from his face.

"I know, Sam," he said out loud. "It's a lie. I am not fine. I'm a wreck and I don't know how to go on each day without you."

The phone buzzed again. John walked out of the bedroom and walked into the kitchen. He opened the freezer and stared at the bottle of vodka. The bottle was a reminder to him of all he had done . . . not that he could ever forget. He had not touched the bottle since the funeral. If only he hadn't touched it before then . . . John had fought the same fight every morning for more than 3 years. He had been to AA meetings, but he had never spoken. He left the FBI after the incident. He looked where his PI license hung on the wall and scoffed.

If you watched TV in the 1980's, you would think every other street in every city had a private investigator on it. What TV didn't tell you was the majority of the work included process serving, chasing down debtors, and, of course, spying on a spouse that someone thinks is cheating. Oh that was the best; all of the training John had received at EKU and Quantico wasted. There was nothing like renting some seedy hotel room and getting some interesting pictures of some not-so beautiful people doing things with other not-so beautiful people. John shook his head in disgust of the mental image that had invaded his mind.

With the type of work he did alone, it was a miracle he had been sober over the last three years. The thought of those people just then was enough to drive most sane men to drink. John barked a laugh at the joke his life and his investigative skills had become. John stared at the bottle and tears welled up in his eyes. "Blast it, Sam! I'm . . ." He was interrupted by a pounding on the door. John knew who it was without even looking out the peep hole in the door. He knew once Chet started in on him, there was no stopping him. He knew that for some reason, known only to Chet, it was time for them to talk. John wiped the tears from his eyes, shut the freezer door, sighed, and headed toward the door.

Chapter 2

The pounding on the door continued. "John! John! Are you in there? I will break down this door! JOHN!" John stared at the door. He peered through the peep hole to see his best friend . . . well, his only friend. Chet looked furious. John stood there thinking of his options. It was early. Well, it was 2 in the afternoon, but it was early for him. He hadn't slept much from the PI case he had just finished working . . . and, honestly, he slept as little as possible for the past three years to avoid dreaming about Sam. His mind wasn't thinking very clearly due to the lack of sleep. John did not think he was in good enough physical shape to try to climb down the fire escape. Well, that was a lie. He was in shape; he just didn't want to exert himself if it wasn't warranted. While John really didn't want to deal with Chet right that second; to climb down a rusty fire escape, which might collapse in the process, seemed a little extreme.

John realized he had to do something soon. Chet was a member of the FBI, so John was pretty sure Chet could actually kick in the door and get away with it. "JOHN!" John sighed and opened the door to face his friend. Chet barged past him and straight into John's bedroom. John knew an explosion was seconds away. John counted down from three on his fingers. When his fingers reached zero, he heard, "WHAT THE? Why does it say Mommy on your cell phone? That's how you list me in your phone?"

John sat down on the couch and smiled. "Good to see you too, Chet. What can I do for you this morning?"

"Why? Why do I bother?" Chet stormed around the living room while John tried to suppress a smirk. "My last girlfriend told me that the best thing I could do is to let you fall into whatever deep depression filled hole it is that you want to! She told me that all you want to do is join Sam. I

8

told her that she was wrong. I told her that you were just going through a rough spot and you would get through it. I broke up with this girl because of the things she said about you! Do you realize that John? I left her because of YOU! Do you know how hot she was?"

John had been trying to hold back the laughter, but the last statement by Chet had pushed him over the edge. John roared with laughter. He laughed until his sides hurt. As he looked through the tears that were rolling out of his eyes he noticed Chet was sitting on the chair laughing as hard as he was.

After several minutes of laughter, and when the chuckles died down, John spoke. "You're the only person that cares about me, Chet, that's why I named your cellphone number Mommy." John tried to keep a straight face but he burst into laughter and Chet did the same. As the laughter finally subsided, John noticed a folder Chet was holding.

"Bring me a present, Chet?" John asked. Chet would sometimes throw things John's way that the FBI couldn't, or didn't want to, touch. Chet hesitated. In that instant John read Chet's face and knew what was in his hand. Oh crap, thought John. "No! No! I am done with the FBI!" John was furious.

"Now, John, calm down. You are being brought on as a consultant only."

"Chet, I have no interest." John replied.

"John, look, I know you don't need the money . . . Oh crap, I'm so sorry." John looked away. Sam had a trust that was left to her by her grandparents. Her grandparents were the only members of Sam's family that John believed liked him. Honestly, her grandparents were stinking, filthy, rich. John had no idea how much money they had; he honestly thought it was billions. All of Sam's trust had been left to John. He didn't know how much was exactly in the trust, but he knew it was enough for him to live five lives on.

Chet opened the folder in front of John. He laid out four pictures of people that had been shot perfectly in the head. John tried to ignore the pictures but the shots were right in the center of each forehead. The pictures had John's interest. Chet let John look. The case would sell itself and Chet knew that. Chet just had to wait and John would hook himself. As John leaned back, seeming to lose interest, Chet reeled him in with one little sentence.

"They were all shot by the same person, within five seconds of each other." Chet said casually. John's eyebrow shot up, and Chet knew he had his best friend back on the hunt with him.

Two Weeks Earlier
1600 Pennsylvania Avenue Washington DC.

Chapter 3

Agent Luke McDonald tried to steady himself as he stood at the first lady's door. "Get ahold of yourself man. She's not going to go off on you . . . I hope."

Luke knocked on the door and waited for the First Lady, Lisa Nichols, to answer. The door opened and Agent McDonald handed a manila envelope to her. "Mrs. Nichols, this has to do with one of those names you asked me to flag in the system." Confusion spread across Mrs. Nichols face. "Those special five names you asked me to flag, ma'am?"

Mrs. Nichols smiled her best campaign smile and took the envelope. Agent McDonald spoke, "I'll double check on the other four names you asked me to keep an eye on." The agent looked down and then back at her. "Mrs. Nichols . . . Lisa . . . I don't know what to say. I'm sorry." For a second Lisa's smile faltered and she looked down at the envelope, confused. Understanding began to spread over her face. She looked sharply at the agent, pursed her lips, and nodded her head in acceptance. The agent nodded and walked away.

As he walked down the hallway and heard the door to Lisa's office close, Agent McDonald thought to himself, "There's a reason I suggested they give her the codename Silk. She's as smooth as they come."

The first lady, or Lisa as she is known to her friends, walked into her private office. "Steady girl." she said to herself.

She opened the envelope and her worst fears were confirmed. The headline to the paper that was photocopied read, **Captain Jason Sparks Dies in Overseas Operation in Afghanistan.** Memories came rushing back to Lisa. Feelings she had repressed for so long . . . they came rushing back as well. She shook her head as if trying to remove them from her mind. "Get a grip." she said to herself. She gripped the sides of her desk. She told herself there was no way anyone could connect the dots on what happened all those years ago.

The fears that she thought she had mastered welled up in her stomach. Her mouth filled with the bitter taste of bile. Tears came to Lisa's eyes but she fought them away. She got up and walked downstairs to find Agent McDonald. Lisa found him in the intelligence center. "Agent McDonald, can you do me a favor?" she asked.

"Of course." he said.

"I need you to check the incoming mail for any of those last four names. I need you to make sure as few people see anything that is sent in from them as possible. Do you understand?"

"Of course, ma'am. Are you expecting something from them?" Luke asked. Lisa shrugged. Luke nodded. "As usual, we will keep this to ourselves?" he asked.

The first lady nodded, smiling.

"Lisa, shall I destroy anything I might find?"

"Agent McDonald," the first lady said smiling. "That is why you are my favorite."

The Next Day
Cemetery just outside of Fort Dunn, New York

Chapter 4

Leroy looked across the cemetery and shook his head. Four people he never thought he would see again were present. The first one he saw was Colt. Colt had his tan from all those years working in Florida at a huge theme park. Every now and then Leroy received letters from Colt. Colt always seemed fine.

Leroy looked back to scan the crowd and saw another familiar face. There was Amy. He thinks her last name is Jensen now. Leroy chucked to himself. Amy sent him a Christmas card every year. The card is always a picture of her, her husband, and two dogs. Leroy thinks she's a second grade school teacher in Illinois.

Of course there was Doctor Tom Bradley of Vermont, the genius of the group. Leroy was always inviting him down for the summer, but Tom never took him up on the offer. Truth be told, he never responded to any of the letters Leroy sent. Leroy had wondered if any of them would respond to the invitation now with Jason's death.

Lastly, there was the quarterback . . . in the casket. He was the reason they were there. Jason Sparks, 2nd Lieutenant, US Army. Leroy looked at the coffin and felt the sadness sweep through him. Lieutenant Sparks was killed in Afghanistan during a hush-hush mission.

Leroy remembered all of the times Jason had protected him in middle school. He really was one of the good guys . . . well except for that little secret that all of them shared. As the funeral went on, he looked around to see if the last member of the group was there.

Veronica Staples was nowhere to be seen. He knew she wasn't there, of course. How could she be? Veronica couldn't be here. She couldn't take the chance that someone might figure it all out; that someone might connect the dots Leroy knew were unconnectable. That's all he had heard from the other three all week. He wasn't surprised. He wondered how many of them secretly were happy she hadn't come.

There were plenty of ways for Veronica to be at the funeral and no one would ever figure out the connection, but . . . no . . . no she couldn't. She couldn't risk the secret they all shared coming out. He understood; he just didn't like it. Of course, with Jason dead, maybe it was time. Maybe the truth could finally come out and he could get a decent night's sleep for the first time in over twenty-five years.

After the funeral and the family left the cemetery, the four of them gathered around the gravesite. No one said much. How could they? They all looked down at their friend. Leroy wondered if all of the thoughts about telling the truth were going through their minds as well. Was it time to tell what really happened all those years ago?

A light snow began to fall. As they stood there, they saw a figure approach them. It dawned on Leroy as the figure was less than 10 feet away who it was . . . but that was impossible. It was just . . . impossible.

Leroy swallowed, "David? David George, is that . . . you?"

"Leroy Jenkins, Amy Jensen, Colt McCormick, Tom Bradley . . ." All four looked nervous and anxious. In one motion, the man in front of them reached down pushing his trench coat aside on both sides of him. Shock and surprise was on all four of their faces as he pulled out a gun in each hand. There were silencers on the end of each gun and they were pointed at the two members of the group on the outside. Simultaneously he shot from both hands and then changed targets to the two on the inside and shot again at the second pair of targets. All four dropped dead. As he fired the shots, he answered.

"Yeah, it's me; David George. You see when I kill someone; I make sure they're dead." David dropped a note on the bodies and then turned and walked away. Each body lay on the ground with a single gunshot wound in the middle of their forehead. The note simply read, "Tell Veronica I know who she is, and she's next."

Now
John Fowler's Apartment, New York, New York

Chapter 5

"Four shots in 5 seconds; how do you know that?" John asked.

Chet smiled. "He sent us a tape of it. He's that good. No one saw it happen. John, he wants us to know who he is."

John looked at the file; it was very thin. He groaned inwardly and looked at Chet. Chet was looking everywhere but in John's eyes. "Chet?"

"Okay, okay. We've got nothing, except there are four people dead and the killer sent us a video. There is also a good chance that the killer . . ." John leaned forward and was staring daggers into Chet. "I mean we feel like there is evidence . . ." John leaned in even closer. "All right; I've got a gut feeling." John fell back on the couch with his arms spread. "John, I really, really think that whoever killed these four people also killed the soldier."

John stared up at the ceiling. Chet was a computer genius. He probably could have been a rich computer tycoon or a world class hacker . . . or both! Chet's biggest problem within the FBI was that he was always looking for a conspiracy. Chet, however, tended to be right about when he had a "feeling" on a case or what seemed to be unrelated cases. That kind of gut instinct had the tendency to ruffle some feathers. Not John, he had no problem looking at something wild and outlandish, he just needed some evidence to back it. That's probably why he and Chet had become so close over the years.

John was lying back against the couch, staring at the ceiling. "Special Forces?"

Chet, "We're pretty sure."

John, "Why?"

Chet looked confused, "Why what?"

"Why do you think this person has Special Forces training?" John asked.

Chet responded. "Four shots in five seconds; you don't learn that on the street. Also, there were some companies deployed in Afghanistan during the time Jason Sparks was stationed there. "

John shook his head. He looked at his friend. "Chet, you're doing it again; you are trying to make the evidence fit a theory. You know better." Chet looked down. He didn't know how many times over the years he had heard the same speech. He couldn't help himself, when he got these gut feelings . . . sometimes they would just take him over, and he would push until he found the mystery. "Hey Chet," John said. "I never said it was a bad theory, but let's let the evidence get us there. Now, since you've headed down this path, let's take it a step further. Is there anyone AWOL who might have this type of training?"

Chet shook his head. "Not that I can find."

John looked at his friend and asked the question that had been troubling him, "Why me?"

Chet froze. John tried hard to repress a slow smile. He knew what was going on. This was a gray area case. Locals didn't want it because of the proximity to the base. Feds didn't really want it because it had loose military ties, and military couldn't investigate because it wasn't military personnel shot at the grave-site. The FBI wanted someone they knew, but wasn't connected directly to them. It was the old political game that he had seen many times . . . and hated.

John also knew what this case meant. It could be a career maker or breaker. If he took this case, it could be his chance back in, but if he couldn't solve it, he would probably never be back with the FBI. John wasn't sure how he felt about that. On one hand he really didn't want back in, but on the other . . . John had never seen the case file on his wife's death. In fact, it was still listed as unsolved. John wanted one thing in his life more than anything, to wrap up that case. He believed he should be in jail, but he was found innocent of all wrongdoings. That means there was more to the story than he knew. As much as he didn't want to join up again, there was that part of him, the part that made him the guy that solved more cold cases, or cases everyone thought were unsolvable, that wanted back in. If the FBI thought it was someone else who had killed Sam . . . John knew this was his one chance. He couldn't appear eager. He had to make them think he was doing them a favor.

John looked at Chet. Chet had turned away trying to think of a polite, political way to answer his question. Chet was struggling with what to say to him.

"Chet, give me one good reason to take this case, just one."

Chet looked his friend straight in the eye, "John, if you ever, ever, EVER want back in, this will be your ticket."

"Why, Chet? Why would I ever want to go back to them? Why . . ." John stopped and looked out the window. It had been over three years and it was still a fresh wound. Because of them . . . because of the FBI, he had lost Sam. This is why he didn't want the case. John swallowed and looked at his friend. John asked the question he had avoided asking for three years.

"Chet," John asked trying to choke back tears, "do you think I'm suicidal?"

Chet was taken aback, "John, where did that come from? Are you trying to tell me something?"

John waved his friend off. "No, nothing like that. I just wondered if you were trying to keep me busy by showing me there is more to life, or showing me the "good" part of the FBI. You know what happened. Chet, you've seen the file. I haven't even seen the official file on her! You're the only person I've ever told what happened to Sam. Not her parents, friends, or anyone. Well that's not entirely true, is it?"

Chet looked away very uncomfortably. John smiled. "How about this? You're the only human I ever told what happened to Sam. For crying out loud, Chet, it's been three years and they've never done anything to me about it!" John looked at his friend. Chet was so uncomfortable. But there was something else, that he couldn't quite put his finger on it. That was one of the things that got John so far in the FBI and made him such a great PI. He noticed the little things and followed the trail until not only was it cold, but there were no other possible leads. Today John had other things on his mind or he might have followed his instincts. "But never mind all of that; you're avoiding the question. Do you think I'm suicidal?"

"No, John," the woman said who had entered the room during the previous exchange and stood quietly leaning against the doorframe. "No, John, you may be vain, arrogant, narcissistic, a pain-in-the-butt, and most importantly very hurt and lonely, but no . . . you're not suicidal."

John looked stunned. He couldn't believe his eyes. The one person he had gone out of his way to avoid more than his in-laws. He stared at the woman and then back at

Chet. "Chet," John said very angrily, "Why on Earth is this woman in my home?"

Chapter 6

"Jessica. What are you doing in MY apartment?!" John bellowed.

Jessica rolled her eyes, straightened up, walked further into the apartment, and looked around. It was in much better shape than she expected. To be honest, it was pretty well kept for an almost forty, recovering alcoholic, widower. She was sure there would be pizza boxes, hamburger wrappers, and the like strewn all around. In fact, truth be told, his apartment was in much better shape than her apartment. Jessica chuckled inwardly. Jessica looked over at John and thought, so far, so good.

Jessica "The Hammer" Hammerstein was probably the one person John hated the most in this world . . . well . . . the second. The first being whoever had killed Sam. Jessica had been given the nickname "The Hammer" because of her work in interrogation. Most criminals always wanted her in the box. Most simply thought she was a beautiful woman that got the job because of her looks. However, once the interview started, they quickly regretted that decision. If Jessica found one inconsistency in an interview, she would hammer on a person until she got that person to break. Every once in a while a story was inconsistent for very valid reasons. Either way, by the time she was done, she would know why. John had used her skills as an interrogator many times over the years.

John spoke, "I'm waiting." Jessica looked at John and took a deep breath.

"John, let's get this out in the open right now. If you're mad at me for what happened in that interview room over three years ago, then you're a fool!" John's mouth fell open. Chet had known this moment was coming, but winced anyway. This moment had been building for three years. He knew if John was to ever come back to the FBI, this moment had to happen. Over three years ago, when

John's wife died, John was a suspect. It was simple really; wife found dead, husband is the first person looked at, end of story. After the biggest Mafia bust in recent FBI history, with John being the lead undercover agent, the FBI had to make absolutely sure their man hadn't gone nuts and taken out his wife.

"John, if the FBI had put anyone else in that box to interrogate you, what would you honestly say? " John said nothing; he just stared at the floor. Jessica continued. "John? John!"

"Cover-up," John whispered.

"John, I can't hear you."

John shot Jessica a death look. He cleared his throat, "A cover-up. I would say the FBI had gone soft and had done a cover-up. I know that Jessica. I accept that. The FBI actually did me a favor by having you grill me. Let me take that back. You didn't grill me; you rode me hard and put me up wet." Chet covered his mouth with his hand so John wouldn't see him smile. "I told you what happened, every gory, blasted detail at least ten different times. So tell me this, Hammer." John said sarcastically. "Why didn't I serve any time for killing my wife?"

Chet grabbed John's arm. "John, we've talked about this." John pulled his arm away and walked to the window and looked out. He put both hands on the window seal and spoke.

"Look, do me a favor, both of you. Get OUT!"

Jessica walked up to John, grabbed him by the shoulders and looked him straight in the eye. "I'm sure Sam loves the way you're keeping her memory." John looked as though he had been slapped. "She's dead, buried, in the ground for three plus years. Get over yourself!" John pulled away and walked out the door of his apartment into the hallway.

Chet started to walk after him and Jessica stopped him.

"Don't. He's got to get past this if we're going to be a team again. I admit, we need him, but we need the old John, not this depressed shell that's living here. Let's start on the file."

"Here?" Chet asked.

"Have you got somewhere more pressing to be?" Jessica asked. "Besides he's got to come back sometime . . . right?"

Chapter 7

John was halfway down the building stairs when it dawned on him; he had just stormed out of his own apartment. He couldn't help it. He began laughing. There were so many emotions that were swirling inside of him. He still didn't know if his friend thought he was suicidal. John knew he wasn't . . . not yet. He had one thing he had to do, and then . . . John pushed those thoughts from his mind. What would Sam say to him if he were to take his own life?

John walked out the door of his building with tears streaming down his face. He walked over two buildings and started up the stairs to his PI Office. Why he kept it he had no idea. It wasn't like he needed all the room. He could do everything in his apartment, but John didn't feel right bringing all of the cases to his home. He needed to keep things separate . . . well as far as PI work was concerned.

Sam use to give him grief constantly for bringing FBI work home. That was all in good fun. It was the undercover work that was the strain on her. Fourteen months planted into the Mafia, John had become too ingrained. He drank with them constantly. He had a problem, but he couldn't do anything until his undercover work was over. John truly was surprised in the last three years no one in the Mafia had tried to take him out. Of course maybe that hadn't happened because they were much too busy trying to take out the "rats" that had turned on the family. As much as some of the Mafia life was romanticized, when it came time to do life, or take a deal and live in witness protection, the mob crumbled. There was also another reason. Maybe the mob thought he was already dead.

John sat at his desk and looked out the window. He could see the building that Sam used to work in. He leaned forward and opened the drawer where he had the locket he had never given Sam. He was going to her the night she died to apologize. They had made all the busts . . . except one. A low level member had gotten away. If John had known that at the time ... John shook his head, tears welling in his eyes. He was going home that night to tell Sam he was joining AA and even quit the FBI if she wanted. John was a block from the apartment when it exploded. The FBI reported John dead. They tried to put him in witness protection, but he refused. That was when he first heard the mutterings of him being suicidal. Maybe he was, or maybe he just felt like he had nothing left to lose.

"Ok, Sam. I take this case, get reinstated, and find your killer. Of course, as far as I'm concerned he's sitting right here in this office." John lowered his head and wept openly. "Sam," he whispered. "Sam, I'm so sorry. It should have been me."

Chapter 8
One Hour Later

John entered his apartment. Jessica and Chet were going through the relatively thin file for a quadruple homicide. Jessica saw John, stood, and walked over to him. She stopped an arm's length away.

"John, we need to finish the conversation we were having," said Jessica. John nodded, his cheeks still wet from tears.

"John, I need you. You haven't lived in over three years, you've just existed. I need one of the FBI's top investigators." Jessica stared at the floor. She spoke very quietly, "John, Chet and I haven't done so well since you left."

John looked up sharply. He glanced over at Chet. John studied him hard. Chet looked a little gaunt in the face. His eyes were puffy and dark like he hadn't been sleeping. John cursed himself under his breath. He had been so wrapped up in his other problems that he hadn't even noticed. He looked back at Jessica and studied her carefully. She was as beautiful as ever, but normally she was also very meticulous about her clothes. When he looked over them, they looked slightly wrinkled. It could have been anything from not being ironed to sleeping in them. Whatever it was, it was something that John, no not John, not this John. John Fowler, FBI agent, he would have noticed. He looked back at Jessica, nodding for her to continue.

"Since you . . . left, our little team has never found a person to replace you. She crossed her arms and slowly started to walk the room. "See . . . well, they kept trying to replace you. Geez I can't believe I'm about to say this."

John crossed his arms and smiled broadly, "I'm waiting."

Jessica turned toward John her face angry. She crossed the space between them in three long strides, her arm extending. She pointed furiously at John as she spoke. "See! See! This is why! This is why no one has contacted you in three years! They don't want to put up with you and your egotistical . . ."

John interrupted her, "Good to see you still can't admit you need and want me."

John ducked to avoid the right hook. Now if someone had walked in on this, they would have thought John was under attack. John knew better. For some reason, and John thought he knew why, he could push Jessica's buttons until she was literally ready to knock his head off. In the seven years they had worked together he had dodged dozens, if not hundreds of punches.

John was laughing, "Ok, ok. Things aren't going good, but you guys survived without me for fourteen months when I was undercover. I mean I was in a little, but mainly it was just the two of you. What has gone so wrong this time?" John smiled at the unspoken question he didn't dare ask at this point.

Jessica was still mad. She was pointing at him and muttering under her breath, "don't you dare." John put his hands up to try and calm her. She sighed and began. "During those fourteen months, no one was put with us. The three of us were a team, and no one dared try to replace you. After you left, well, the politics started."

John looked at the floor. So this was his fault as well. Ten years ago the three of them started working together on a case and closed what was not only thought to be a cold case, but impossible under most circumstances, in other words; a career maker. The three had been made a permanent team. They became the go to team on all big cases. Chet could handle any computer problems, John could sniff out any lead, and Jessica could get the location of Hoffa's body out of the person who buried him if she had him in the box . . . or out of the box. But that was a different story for a different day. John always worried what would happen to them if they were separated. Each of them was a perfectly good agent, but they each had a label. Like actors in Hollywood feared being typed cast, John had feared that each member would only be seen as their strengths, not as a total agent. Now John's fears for the team had come true.

John looked at Jessica, "Trip?"

Jessica nodded. Lionel Pennyworth Smothers III, or known as Trip, at his insistence not the agents' choice, was the Director of the New York office. John sat down in the chair. He looked up at Jessica waiting for the next shoe to fall. Jessica sat on the couch across from him.

"Bruce?" John asked. Jessica nodded slowly. John slumped in the chair. Bruce had been the go to guy in the office before John arrived in the New York Office. Bruce had told John many times he was going to enjoy watching him go all the way back down the ladder. According to Bruce, John had stepped on everyone's head on the way up the ladder. John hadn't, he had just taken Bruce's spot; a spot that was thought to have been arranged by Bruce's father, a US senator. John knew differently, but that was a story for a different day.

"So if you don't solve this one . . ." John began. Jessica was nodding as he began speaking. John just left it hanging.

"Bruce has convinced the brass in Washington that we aren't complete agents. He's convinced them we are only good as the team, and now, without you, we can't be complete. He has completely convinced Washington that being on the team has hurt us. And Trip . . . well Trip can't fight Washington and Bruce knows it." Jessica said.

28

John leaned forward and put his head in his hands. Trip was a good guy; he just wasn't one to stick his neck on the line. He wanted a safe, comfortable job. John was willing to take chances. Many had worked over the years, but some had backfired . . . very, very badly. If the higher-ups at Washington were leaning on him . . . well, why would Trip save them? For that matter, how could Trip save them? Actually there was no them right now, was there . . .

John raised his head up, "So you believe if I come back and help you, then you will have kept yourselves safe for now? Let's say I do this, we figure it out and solve this case. What happens next time? This is a one-time reunion. We're not putting the band back together."

Jessica smiled. "John, help us and buy us a few months. After this case is over and you don't want back in, I'll drop it." Chet shot Jessica a look and started to speak. She put her hand over his mouth and shushed him. Jessica continued to talk with her finger over Chet's mouth which caused John to raise his eyebrows. "If you help us, win or lose, Trip has agreed to let you see the file."

John was about to ask if her and Chet had become an item, but with this revelation John jumped to his feet.

"Jessica, Chet . . . do not play with me!" John was trying hard to keep his composure. This was what he wanted, and more importantly, needed.

Jessica walked up to him and took both of his hands in hers. She looked straight into his eyes. He had seen that look once before. It was during the interrogation. "John, I need you to be you. You need to live again. You need to be that . . . " She looked up at the ceiling, blew out a breath and continued, "you need to be that arrogant, cocky," John's grin was growing by the second and irritation was slowly spreading its way across Jessica's face. "smug, narcissistic, jerk that can follow a 10 year old scent across three continents." Jessica was staring hard into John's eyes.

John broke the silence. "I know exactly what you are thinking." Jessica raised an eyebrow. John continued. "You're thinking, he's a widower now, and he has been for three years, would it be inappropriate if I kiss him?"

Jessica threw down John's hands, and stood up as straight as she could to look him in the eye. She spoke softly but very crisply. "You know I asked Sam once about your obsession with me." John was taken aback. "She said I was the only woman she ever worried about. I told her then she had absolutely nothing to worry about. Nice to see you're back . . . Jerk!"

Jessica turned to walk away, but John grabbed her arm. She slowly turned looking at the hand on her arm and then at John.

"Jessica . . . I'm sorry." Irritation left Jessica's face. "Jess . . . I . . . was so mad at you . . . you just did your job. I was so wrapped up . . . "

Jessica stopped him. "John, it's okay. It wasn't your fault. I was too proud to call you and see how you were. Look we've all made mistakes. Let's just do what the three of us do best and crack this case. OK?"

John nodded. Jessica paused and then spoke, "There is one thing." John looked at her. "You will be a consulting agent." John nodded. "And if I hear you once refer to yourself as a murderer or having killed Sam during this case, I won't miss the punch on purpose. Understand?"

John smiled and turned to head out the door. "Let's head over to my office, and Jess, the answer is yes. . . ." Jessica looked confused. "It would be inappropriate for you to kiss me." John turned and walked out. Chet hurried after him. Jessica smiled. Yeah, enough of him was back, for now. As much as she hated to admit it, she needed all of him back. She needed John back in the FBI or she and Chet were goners, but first things first. They had to solve this murder or there would be no second chance for any of them.

Chapter 9

The three of them entered John's PI office. John sat down at his desk and Chet placed each picture of the victims on the evidence board John kept in the room. After all four pictures were up, he looked at John. John smiled and nodded. Chet placed the fifth picture on the board . . . Captain Jason Sparks, United States Army. Jessica stood back and smiled. John noticed.

"What?" John asked.

"It's like you never left," said Jessica. "You're supposed to be a consultant and yet here you are running the show again." John started to get up, and Jessica held up her hand. "No, don't. I'm not mad. Chet and I had a week on this our way, you run it. Just remember when we get in the field you have little to no authority. In fact let's go with no authority so there aren't any questions down the road."

John nodded. "Jessica, if I overstep my bounds, I have no worry that you will gladly put me in my place." Jessica smiled and looked down. Chet looked away, uncomfortable. "Ok, time for me to ask a question to make everyone uncomfortable." Chet looked quite confused. "Chet, Jessica, are you two currently a thing? Before you get all defensive, remember who I am and what I can do. I'm not that addled."

Chet had turned fourteen shades of red, and Jessica looked away. That's when it clicked in John's head; the conversation in his living room earlier with Chet. John looked out the window. He then stood up and walked over to it. He stared out the window and spoke quietly.

"I'm batting 1.000 right now aren't I? I caused my wife's death; almost cost you two your careers, and now you two can't even have a relationship because of me. Dear God, what kind of broken am I?"

Jessica walked up behind him. She wanted to comfort him, but that was impossible. John only let one person in his entire life comfort him, and she was gone. Chet had tried to be his friend, and he was . . . as much as John would let him. Jessica straightened and started to speak but John looked at her. His eyes were dancing with mischief through the tears.

"So which is the lie? The one you told me today, or the one you told Chet when he left you?"

Admittedly John's detective skills were a little rusty, but he flat missed the cut sign that Chet was flashing over and over.

"Excuse me?" Jessica exclaimed. "He left me! Wait; when I walked in earlier . . . He said I thought you were suicidal? He was the one . . . " Jessica realized what John had just done. "You Jerk!" John was grinning like a Cheshire cat. He now had his answer. Chet thought John was suicidal. He also knew that Jessica had left Chet, and she left him because of Chet's worry over him. John walked over to the board and faced both his partners.

"Look there was a time when no one thought we could crack what was supposed to be an impossible case. We did. We did it as a team with no secrets. Chet, I don't know, maybe I am suicidal." Chet nodded. John may have kept Chet away as much as possible, but he was still an FBI agent, and a good one. "Have I thought about it, yeah . . . but how mad would Sam be at me if I did?" Chet looked at John with pity, but John waved it off.

"You want me to get through this? Then help me with this case, and you two promise to help me with one more, if . . . IF I want you to." Chet nodded solemnly. Jessica looked uncomfortable.

"John, it's easy to say all of this, but if Chet and I are kicked out of the FBI how can we help you with Sam's case?" Jessica asked.

John straightened. For the first time in three years, John Fowler felt like himself. The cocky smirk that drove his teammates crazy, but the one that also let them know he was on the hunt, returned. Jessica smiled in spite of herself. For the first time since she and Chet had run into so much trouble at the bureau, things felt right. They were back. John reached over to the hat rack and put on what he called his "crime solving" hat.

"I'm going to help you solve this case and then we're all going to get the redemption we deserve."

Chapter 10

John looked at the board and began to study it. He realized he wasn't getting anywhere. He sighed and turned to his partners.

"I guess it's time I get my comeuppance. We probably need the big board at the bureau plus all of the files you have there." Chet looked embarrassed and Jessica was studying her shoes. John was a little taken aback. "OK. Exactly how bad is it at the bureau?"

Jessica was playing with the top button on her shirt. She wet her lips before she spoke. "We were only given this case two days ago." John's mouth dropped. Jessica held up her hand. "It wasn't our fault, it took almost a week for jurisdiction to be decided and it took a few days for everyone else in the department to have their take on the case." John had a bad feeling he knew where this was going. It was obvious they weren't going to come right out and say, so he asked.

"You weren't assigned this case, were you? You went to Trip and asked for it, and asked for me to take a run on it? That's what this whole thing is? You put your careers on the line? Admittedly, not that it sounds like much is left of them at this point." Both Chet and Jessica looked a little hurt with that statement. At this point John didn't care. He was on a roll and couldn't help himself. "You two numbskulls gambled everything that, A, you could get me to come back, and B, and this is the doozy, that I wasn't so drunk or so rusty that I could solve a quadruple homicide that's now over two weeks old?

"I didn't think you had been drinking." Chet had been quiet during most of the exchanges that afternoon. He had taken about all he could though. Whether John wanted him or not, Chet was John's friend. He had to do something to try to save John's life. Chet figured his FBI career was over anyway. He was willing to gamble with

35

what little he had left for one big win. John started to speak and Chet cut him off. John was a little surprised by the ferocity shown by his friend.

"John, for three years I've let you push me away, but no more. Look at the evidence in front of you." John looked puzzled and glanced at the board. "No you idiot, not the board, YOU!" John was very taken aback. "In a couple of hours, after not doing any real investigative work over the past three years, you have figured out almost every secret we have kept from you. John, your mind makes these connections that the rest of us can't. So maybe you're only 60 to 75% of the old John. Who cares? Don't you get it? You were, and still are, one of the best. Your best guess is better than absolute certainties of ¾ of the agents I have worked with!"

John looked around the room. "You know I do work very hard on my investigations as a PI." Chet looked on in irritation and Jessica started to snicker. "You know how hard it is on some of these stakeouts not to eat myself out of my pant size or break down and drink?" Chet was fighting back a smile, and Jessica's snickering was louder. A slow grin was crossing John's face. "And do you know how hard it is for me to not to lose my lunch on some of the photographs . . ."

Jessica cut him off, laughing. "Okay, you have worked hard."

John stopped laughing and looked down. "No, I haven't. I've just existed." Jessica gave him an understanding smile. "Can I even get back in the building?" Jessica handed him a pass. "Ok, so we need to go there. Look, it's late; let's start fresh in the morning. Chet can you pull all the electronic files on these folks and print them off for me?" He raised his hand before Chet could say anything. "I know, I can look online, but sometimes with the printouts in my hands I can see the connections better." Chet nodded. "So what time tomorrow?"

Jessica smiled; she had been waiting for this all day. "8 AM." John looked hurt. "You can be up by then, right?" John knew he had been bested. He gave her a smile. Jessica waved at both men and walked out. John turned to his friend, but Chet spoke first.

"Before you say anything, John, she was a beautiful girl that I worshiped . . . but I don't know if I loved her or if I even had the kind of feelings she needed me to have for her."

John looked away. "I know, Chet. You kind of said it earlier." Chet looked confused. "You said 'do you know how hot she was?' not 'do you know how much I liked, or even loved, her?'." Chet smiled and shook his head. He then grabbed John in a bear hug. John was taken aback and then gave the most awkward hug imaginable. Chet pulled away and slapped his friend on the arm.

"John, that's why I didn't give up on you; you're the best. Even as narcissistic as you are," John feigned shock, "you can't admit how good you really are." Chet paused. "Three things and I'll leave." John nodded. "The first, and most important, Sam's death is not your fault." John looked at the ground. "John I mean it. Solve this case and you can have the file. With that file you can find out exactly what I mean." John looked up, face determined and nodded. "Second, she would want you to move on." Chet held up his hand before John could speak. "Hear me out. I know you, you need to finish this, but Sam would want you to find someone else . . . even Jessica." Both men smiled and Chet headed toward the door.

"Chet," John called after him. "What was the third thing?"

Chet replied without missing a step, "That woman is crazy about you, and part of me honestly believes she only dated me to get closer to you."

Chet continued out the door and was gone. John looked around the room and began to tidy up. He put all the papers and pictures back into their files. He looked around to make sure he hadn't missed anything, packed up and headed out the door. As he walked back to his apartment and felt the chill in the February air, he thought about doing something different tonight. Maybe he would watch some college basketball. He hadn't watched a ball game in a couple of years now. Maybe he'd get lucky and his Cats would be on. He stood on the sidewalk and looked up at the skyline. Maybe the healing was finally beginning. All he knew is for the first time in three plus years, he didn't want a drink.

Chapter 11

As John entered the NY offices of the FBI all he could think about was how desperately he wanted a drink. He knew it would be bad, but he had no idea it would be . . . well, nothing could prepare him for this. And to think the morning had gone so well.

John woke up at 5 am, and made himself presentable. He then looked in the mirror and decided to go for dapper. The problem with that is the only good suit he still had was the suit he had worn to the funeral three years ago. After several minutes of deliberating, John decided to wear it. After all, he could very well be going to the burial of his FBI career if this didn't work out right. John exited his apartment and headed back to what used to be his office.

When he walked up to security, there stood Fred. Fred's jaw dropped and he ran over to hug John. John had seen Fred's face every day he had worked in the building manning the security booth. After a few pleasantries John headed up to the old office. When he rounded the corner to the section of the offices his group used to occupy, he froze. There was no open space anymore, but a wall. On the door leading into the offices it read Bruce Cosby. John was stunned. He knew Bruce had stroke, but this was absolutely ridiculous. He went over to the offices Bruce and his cronies used to occupy, and he saw all of Bruce's old cronies still had their offices there. Well if Bruce was over there, and his cronies were here . . . oh no.

John hurried to what was called the rookie room. When he looked in the doorway he saw what were obviously new recruits for the NY office. Well, all John knew is they had been there less than three years, because he knew none of them. John put his hand over his face. There was only one place his crew could be, the foxhole. John had renamed the basement the foxhole since most agents that found themselves there were dug in and seemingly fighting for their lives to stay in the FBI.

John was standing in the hall trying to decide what to do. He looked down the hall and saw a light on in Trip's office. Well, he shouldn't have a drink before meeting with the man in charge. John drew in a deep breath and headed for Trip's office. Trip's door was open. John went to knock on the door, and like always, Trip waved him in without ever looking up. It was spooky. John had to watch himself around Trip. Trip was over six foot tall and muscular. He was bald on the top of his head with short hair around the sides. He had been known wear gold wire-rimmed glasses. John always thought Trip looked strange in a suit and tie, but Trip seemed to thrive in his position as director in the New York offices. John walked in and Trip, while still reading a report, opened a drawer and pulled out an official pass with John's picture on it. John took the pass, and clipped it to his coat.

"John, I need you to wear that at all times you're here. Not everyone, like Fred, is still here and knows you." Trip closed the case file he had been reading and leaned back in his chair. He ran his hand over his balding head. He stared at John a second and a slow smile came over Trip's face. He stood up, and walked toward John. John had expected a handshake. He was very surprised when Trip hugged him. Trip stepped back and put one hand on John's shoulder.

"John, I am so glad to see you. As much as you drove me crazy, you're a saint compared to Bruce." John was so stunned by the honesty of Trip that he began to laugh, and then to his surprise, stoic, rock solid Trip, began to laugh out loud. Trip turned and got a refill on his cup of coffee, and offered one to John, who politely declined. Trip leaned back on the coffee counter, took a deep breath and spoke.

"I need to say some things, and I need you not to interrupt me." John nodded. "First, no matter what happens, you will get full access to your wife's file." John swallowed and looked away his eyes moistening. "I would ask you not look at it until you finish with this current case. I know how much that file will mean to you and I know you will put your everything into it, and right now, I have two live agents who need your help. After this case is over, I will give you every available resource I can to help you with that file." Trip stopped. He wanted to let it sink in exactly what he had told John. John shook his head as if to clear cobwebs. He couldn't believe that Trip was willing to go out on a limb for him. Maybe John had misjudged Trip all of these years, or maybe what happened with John and Sam had changed Trip. He didn't know, but he did know he was glad of the change.

Trip continued, "Second," Trip paused, sighed and continued. "I am sorry for having to put Jessica in the box with you that night. If I hadn't, the DOJ would have come after all of us John. I did what I had to do, but I promise you I didn't like it." John nodded.

"Third, if, after this is over, you want back with your team, I will do everything I can to give you your spot back. I must warn you that Bruce has all but built a house in your old office space." John smiled. Who knew that John was less trouble to Trip than Bruce? John waited to make sure Trip was finished and then spoke.

"First . . . Thank you. Second I completely understand, and third, if, and that's one mighty big if," Trip nodded, "if I come back, can my group just keep the foxhole?" Trip nearly choked on his coffee. He stared at John incredulously. Then Trip chuckled and smiled.

"You want to be down there in the basement?" Trip asked. John nodded. Trip continued. "It would kill him to know you're solving cases down there and not on the main floor. He thinks he took something away from you, but if you show it doesn't bother you, that will just kill him." Trip clapped his hands together. "I love it!" John had a huge grin on his face. "It's all yours, and it's perfect! It has everything upstairs did, and Chet actually has more computers down there than he did upstairs." It was John's turn to look stunned.

"I didn't know that was humanly possible," John said. Trip chuckled. John continued, "If you don't mind, sir, I have two agents to help, and possibly a third to get reinstated, but most importantly there's a certain someone here I need to make his life as miserable as possible." Trip laughed and gestured toward the door. John tipped his hat and headed outside. Trip chuckled and drank from his coffee cup. He then spoke out loud.

"I think things may get a little interesting around here over the next few weeks."

Chapter 12

John started downstairs when he heard a mocking voice call out to him.

"So how is the view from the bottom?" John stopped and smiled. He was going to enjoy this one. John turned and walked toward Bruce.

"Bruce," said John, offering out his hand, "so good to see you."

Bruce took John's hand hesitantly. "John, glad to see you. I'm sad to say we have heard some bad rumors around here about you. I'm glad to see they were just rumors."

John smiled and put his hands in his pockets. He rocked back on his heels and nodded his head toward the offices that Bruce now occupied. "I've noticed you've moved up in the world."

Bruce smiled. "I must have impressed several people. I mean they did give me a section of the office that used to hold three people." Bruce was looking very proud of himself. John slapped Bruce on the back and started to walk off. Trip walked out of his office and leaned against the doorframe. John was counting down in his head and as he reached one, Bruce called out. John smiled and turned.

"John! If there's anything I can do to help, you be sure and let me know."

John walked back toward Bruce. "You mean like sitting on a week old case for three days to make sure that my crew, excuse me, I'm not an employee here anymore, my FRIENDS, have almost no chance to solve?" Bruce's smile fell. "I don't think I need that type of help at any point in my life."

Bruce drew himself up and stepped right up into John's face. Trip smiled, if John was 70% of what he used to be, this was going to be all sorts of fun.

"You better watch your step, Boy," Bruce said.

There was a veiled threat in the sound of his voice. John looked amused. Bruce continued, "There's a new top dog around here. Take a good look around." Bruce nodded his head toward his office.

John gave Bruce his second in the sun, and then decided to bring him back down to Earth. "Hey, Bruce, where's your picture with your Dad?" Bruce looked confused. "You know like the THREE he shot with me for the cases I solved? You know the ones that he won his campaign with?" Bruce looked ready to spit nails. "I mean you had three years by yourself to rack up some photo ops and I don't see anything." John started to walk away, but stopped and turned back to Bruce, his voice very soft.

"I don't care if you hate my guts, but understand this, if I was the raging alcoholic agent that you painted me out to be, I would still be five times the investigator that you would ever hope to be. Now if you don't mind, I have a case to help my friends solve. Why don't you go ahead and call Daddy and see if he wants another photo op with me? It's sad, you've yet to realize, that if he didn't take all these pictures with me, he might not get reelected. If he didn't get reelected, you might not have a job." John held his hand up before Bruce could speak. "You see, I know the truth. You father never asked for you to have a single job in his life. Washington has always thought that having you as an agent keeps him happy." John dropped his voice down to a whisper. "Wouldn't they be shocked if they found out how much your father would enjoy it if you lost your cushy FBI gig?"

John turned and walked down the hall, nodding at Trip as he walked by. Bruce had turned a shade of red that was off the color chart. He marched into his office and slammed the door. Bruce's nameplate fell off the door. Trip laughed. It was good to have John back.

John rounded the corner and there stood Jessica, smiling.

"Making friends again, John?" Jessica asked.

"I know I should be the bigger man, but I enjoyed that."

Jessica laughed. "We all did, John. We all did. Now let me lead you to our offices."

John smiled, "I know the way to the foxhole, but I will follow you anywhere." Jessica looked surprised by his deduction of the foxhole, but punched his arm for the last comment. John laughed and started down the stairwell. Jessica sighed. She knew one way or another, things were about to change in the agency.

Interlude
David George

Chapter 13

David George walked into the seedy hotel. He paused for a second trying to remember which alias he had used to rent his room. He silently chided himself for not having a better plan. David knew better than not to have a plan. Ever since he left the service he hadn't planned the way he knew he should. David paused, got a mental grip on himself and remembered the alias. He took a deep breath, and confidently walked up to the front desk and paid for another week's stay. The manager took the money and offered David a receipt. David passed on it and started toward the stairs.

The package he held in his hand was what he had been waiting for. It had been delivered to the PO Box two days ago, but David hadn't sent his runner to get it until this morning. That was the great thing about this town. He could easily find someone who wanted to make $100.00; $25.00 up front and $75.00 upon delivery of the package. The best part was David never had to show his face at the PO Box. David didn't think he was being paranoid, but right now he could care less. In one week he would have Veronica in his sights, and he would do to her what he couldn't all those years ago.

He shook the memories from his head and started up the stairs to his room on the third floor. The hotel was sleazy, there was no doubt about that, but no one cared who he was or why he was here, and that was exactly what he was after right now. He entered his room and opened the package. He had been invited to the White House as part of the dinner honoring the 5th Special Forces Group. David had just finished his last tour of duty three weeks ago. It wasn't supposed to be his last tour. He had planned on re-upping, but David knew he couldn't after what had taken place in Afghanistan. He sat down on the bed, and then laid back. He closed his eyes and the memories started flooding back to him of those last days in Afghanistan. He shook his head trying to get rid of them, but they came unabated and all David could do was relive them, whether he wanted to or not.

Chapter 14

It was pure coincidence he had crossed paths with Jason Sparks in Afghanistan, but as far as David was concerned it was the best luck ever. It was chance that both units were in the same small town in Afghanistan. When David first met members of Jason's unit, he heard someone mention Jason's name. David asked around about Jason; he asked around every time he heard names that could possibly be related to his past. They had always turned out to be people he didn't know in the past, but this time it turned out to be someone he did know. What were the chances of David ever meeting anyone he knew over here?

David couldn't believe it. It was actually the man he knew, Jason Sparks of Kentucky. David thought at first maybe the name was just a coincidence; there had to be several people named Jason Sparks from Kentucky. David did try to keep out of sight as much as possible just in case it was the same Jason he knew. There was no sense taking chances it might be the man he knew. No, it was best to play it safe and deal with it when he verified if it really was Jason. When the fighting broke loose in the streets however, David saw his opportunity he took it.

Jason had gotten separated from his unit by enemy fire. He was pinned down behind a car while taking fire from snipers in a building across the street. When David happened upon the firefight, he couldn't believe his eyes. There was Jason Sparks; how had he gotten from Kentucky to Afghanistan was anyone's guess. The irony of the situation was not lost on David. He had gone thousands of miles away from Kentucky to avoid six people and had found one of them in a small town in Afghanistan. David was assessing the situation when he noticed a member of the Taliban circling Jason and starting to approach him from the back. David was furious, there was no way he had finally found Jason all these years later just to watch another man kill him. He screamed at Jason.

"Behind you!"

Jason turned to see the Taliban member coming toward him. Jason sprayed gunfire toward the enemy soldier. The enemy soldier took cover behind an overturned cart in the road. David signaled he would get the Taliban member behind Jason, while Jason would get the sniper still in the building across the street. David came in behind the Taliban soldier and hit him in the head with the butt of his gun. The Taliban soldier went sprawling, dropping his gun, while Jason shot the sniper across the street. Jason turned around to see if his fellow soldier needed help and saw the US soldier standing over the prone body of his would be assailant. Jason came up toward David with his hand extended. David ignored the hand and bent down to pick up the enemy weapon. Jason was a little taken aback. David spoke before Jason could.

"Jason Sparks . . . from Kentucky?" Jason looked stunned. He really had no idea who was in front of him. David smiled very slowly and asked him the question that would end Jason's life.

"You don't remember me?" Jason shook his head no, looking very confused. "How about my sister?" Jason looked even more confused. "Does the name Beth George ring a bell?" David asked. David watched as realization slowly crept over Jason's face. David felt a slow smile cross his face. He then spoke the last words Jason would ever hear.

"I'm David, David George."

Jason looked as though he saw a ghost, and then dropped dead as David shot him with the enemy weapon. David then picked up his own weapon and shot the Taliban soldier. David felt elated inside as he called for help. As other solders found his position, David had to repress the glee inside. As far as David was concerned what just happened was self-defense. It may have been over 25 years since it was needed, but it was self-defense in his mind all the same.

Chapter 15

David stood up from the bed he had been reminiscing on and walked to the window. He could see the Washington Monument from his window. This was coming together so much better than he could have ever hoped for. He walked over to his closet to inspect his dress uniform. He suspected it would be the last time he ever wore it . . . unless they tried or buried him in it. When this was over, he truly doubted anyone would ever remember that he served his country. David thought back to that awful day when his life had truly changed. The day when Jason had caused him to fall down that old mine shaft and land on top of the lifeless form of his sister.

He thought about how he wanted to go back home, but knew he couldn't. He knew if his mother was alive, she would never forgive him for not protecting his sister. David thought of the irony. His mother never protected him or his sister. They had looked out for each other for years, until Jason had ended her life and tried to end his.

He thought about the old family that had taken him in a few days later. He was nearly dead when they found him. David had found an opening in the old mine shaft he had been shoved down, and crawled out of it. He had hid out in the hills until the old man had found him when he was out hunting. The old man who had helped raise him for the next five years was the closest thing to a father David had ever known.

David shook his head. His mother had little to no education that he knew of. She drank, took all sorts of drugs, and would date any man in the county, or surrounding counties, that wanted her. It was no shock to him when he learned she had died of an OD two months after he and his sister had disappeared. He wanted to go back after his mother died and tell the town what had happened to Beth, his sister, that day . . . but he knew better. He knew Veronica would have something done to him, or worse, no one would believe him over Veronica. No, it was better this way.

Pap, that's what the old man had David call him, raised him. Pap and Maw lived in the hills. Everything they had they got from hunting, farming, or fishing. Every once in awhile, Pap would go into town and buy a few things and get his mail, but for the most part he and Maw lived off of the land. David never learned their last names. Pap worked David hard on the farm. David didn't seem to mind. He immersed himself into the work.

Maw began to home school David. When he started to complain, Maw told David if he wanted any chance of getting in the Army someday he had to have a diploma. Not only did David stop complaining, but he poured as much effort into school as he did with work. Ever since Maw and Pap found David, all he would talk about was joining the Army when he turned eighteen. He believed it was his only chance to get away and not be found by the group; Veronica's group. The one he had tried to be part of . . . until Beth died and Jason tried to kill him. They had never wanted him in the group since he was a few years younger than the rest of them. He always followed them whenever Beth went out with them. After Beth died, he never really thought they were looking for him, but he always wondered. He wondered if anyone checked to make sure that both of them were dead.

When the day came that David turned eighteen, he told both Pap and Maw goodbye. Pap gave David a ride into town, and $200.00. Pap said he had earned that and more over the years. They shook hands and David headed into town to try and find out where the nearest Army recruiter was. Pap watched him walk away and never tried to chase after David. Pap had watched the scrawny broken boy he found grow up to be a very strong and dangerous man. Pap knew something had happened to him, but never asked what. As far as he was concerned it was probably best David joined the Army. Pap drove off, never to be seen by David again, and honestly, Pap never wanted to see David again.

David's biggest fear was when he joined the Army he would be questioned about his disappearance for over six years. David was stunned when everything was over and no one had asked him about him or his sister.

David snapped back to the present. He always wondered why his mother had never filed a missing persons report. As he climbed the ranks of the Army and was stationed at Fort Campbell, he did a little digging. Apparently neither he nor his sister had ever been listed as missing, or dead. Looking back, he couldn't say he was surprised. His mother avoided the law as much as she could. She always suspected the law was after her. What he understood now that he didn't understand as a child is the only reason the local sheriff and police kept looking in on her was to check on him and Beth.

It was a small town he grew up in until the incident and everyone knew that it was really just him and Beth. People in small towns tend to take care of their own. Someone always seemed to be bringing a casserole or something over at night for him and Beth to eat . . . which was good, because Beth really wasn't much of a cook. As bad a cook as she was though, she was a much better cook than David's mother. Beth was probably more of a mom to him than his own mother. Beth . . .over 25 years later, and he still woke up in a cold sweat thinking of that last time he ever saw her before she went to meet Veronica. David set his jaw and nodded to himself. He would see that Veronica came to justice . . . one way or another.

Chapter 16

As John entered the foxhole, he gave a low whistle.
Chet had apparently gotten his hands on every state of the
art piece of technology he could find. There were digital
displays everywhere. Chet was standing over a monitor
moving his hands like something out of a sci-fi movie
looking through different files. John knew his buddy was
good with computers, but maybe John had underestimated
Chet. For the first time John noticed that Chet seemed
confident. This was Chet's element. John knew what he
owed his friend. They had to solve this case. John cleared
his throat, but Chet had him tuned out. John walked over
and laid his hand on Chet's shoulder. Chet turned.

"Everything you asked for, Boss," Chet said. John
shot a quick glance at Jessica who waved the comment off.
Chet started to apologize and Jessica cut him off.

"Chet, stop! This is the most active, happy, and
confident I've seen you since. . ." she glanced over at John,
"Well, since Captain Bozo here left." She pointed her
thumb toward John.

"Captain Bozo? Captain Bozo? You came
crawling back to me," Jessica sighed, and lifted her hands
toward the heavens in exasperation. John continued, "And
you call me Captain Bozo?" John smiled, "That sounds
about right." Jessica smiled. The team was back. John
started to take charge of the investigation.

"Ok, let's start going through everything and see if
we can find a connection. Jessica, where are we on

interviewing spouses of the victims?" John turned toward Jessica who had a sheepish look on her face.

"John . . . see, here's the thing." John sat down. He didn't know what was about to come out of her mouth, but he knew it was going to be nothing good. "Their local PD did the interviews."

"Why would New York PD interview the suspects?" asked John.

"John, when I say local . . . I mean the local PD where the spouses are." John wasn't quite sure what to say. "John, this case is dead cold. We have been authorized to travel to speak to one spouse."

John was livid. "This is a practical joke, right? I mean what is the point?" John was running his hand through his hair in frustration. Jessica was watching him, waiting to give him the rest of the bad news. John noticed Jessica and groaned inwardly. There was more. It was going to get worse. He wasn't sure how that was humanly possible, but it was about to get worse. He waited.

Jessica began. "You see, when I say we are authorized, what I really mean is the FBI will cover the expenses of someone to talk to one spouse and see if there are any leads to follow. If the interview creates new leads, then, and only then, will the FBI consider authorizing more manpower to be placed onto this case." John rubbed his hand slowly down his face. The look on his face was incredulous.

"Exactly what did you two do to get this deep in? You don't have a case; you have a wild goose chase!" John stormed around the room muttering. Chet and Jessica both were snickering at him. "What?"

Jessica responded, "Chet said he knew that would be your reaction to this." Chet was bursting with laughter. John couldn't help but smile. These two knew he hadn't done any real detective work in nearly three years, they had a case that was stone cold dead and they thought he could solve it. It felt good that someone, somewhere, had faith in him.

Chapter 17

John turned back to Chet.

"Show me what you got," John motioned to the numerous displays. Chet jumped at his chance to show off his techno-magic.

"Ok," said Chet. "Tom Bradley lived in Vermont." As Chet spoke he was opening virtual files with speed that was making John's eyes hurt. "Tom was a local doctor there that practiced family medicine. He was married, no kids, no record, and nothing strange on financials." Chet moved to the next digital file. "Amy Jensen, originally Majors, married to Todd Jensen, lives in Illinois, currently a second grade school teacher with two dogs, nothing funny on financials and no record." John held up a hand to stop Chet before he hyperventilated.

"Let me guess," said John. "On the others, there are no records and nothing strange in the financials?" Chet nodded. "Any connections, anywhere?" Chet shook his head no. "Do you have everything printed out?" Chet nodded. "Then I'll go through these by hand and see if I can make any connections on anything." Chet lifted a full banker's box full of files onto the desk. John sighed and sat down. Jessica walked over and sat down next to him.

"John, are you ready for this?" Jessica asked. John looked puzzled, Jessica continued. "This case, John, are you ready to get back into this routine?" The puzzled look left John's face. He turned and looked at Jessica.

"Jess, I need this. I may never be ready for it, but I need this. I'm not upset about having to work a case. I just can't figure out why there isn't one clue anywhere on how any of these four had a link to Captain Jason Sparks. Chet, run him for me."

John hopped up and headed for the display while Chet made the images dance on the screen. "Captain Jason

Sparks. Won a State Football Championship in high school and then joined the Army upon graduation. Jason received many commendations in his Army career and was killed in a firefight in Afghanistan by suspected members of the Taliban."

John looked over the electronic file. There was absolutely nothing. Not one thing that connected these people except four of them were shot and killed at Jason's funeral. That fact itself screamed at John. He didn't know yet what it was screaming, but it was screaming at him all the same. John started to pace. Somewhere these people had to have crossed paths. Four random people did not just suddenly decide to attend a man's funeral that each of them had never met, and then get shot. The chances of that were astronomical. He stopped when he snapped his fingers.

"Chet!" John yelled excitedly, "Check the birth certificates."

Chet cut him off. "Already done, Boss, everyone was born in the current state they were living in."

John dropped his head, but had one last idea. "Chet, what about high schools?"

Chet opened more electronic files. "Sorry, Boss, they all graduated from the state they were born in. Now you are talking mid-to-late 80s for their earlier school records. Many of these records are not stored electronically, and I'm working on finding them, but it's going to take a while."

John was dejected. "Keep on it, you might just find something there. So which one of the victim's spouses do I get to interrogate?"

Jessica spoke up. "It's your call, John, what does your gut tell you?"

Chet pulled up all the pictures of the victims. John looked at each, his gaze kept returning to the Doctor from

Vermont, Tom Bradley. John walked up to the electronic image, and turned to face the other two.

"For some reason," John said pointing toward Tom's picture, "I think this is the one I need to find out about." Jessica was leaning against a desk with her arms crossed. She smiled and uncrossed them. She looked John straight in the eyes.

"Then go to Vermont, John, and find out what you can about our Doctor and his connection to this group. And for our sake, please do it fast. I'm not sure how much colder this case can get before it is gone forever." John nodded and turned back to look at Tom's picture. Something in his gut told him he would find something there. As John stood there, he could feel something building in him he hadn't felt in a long time . . . hope. He had no idea why. Then it dawned on him. He was back on a case, and felt no urge for a drink, and for the first morning in the past three years, he wasn't heartbroken about Sam. He still missed her, but the numbness he felt inside each time he thought of her wasn't there. Yes it was definitely hope he felt. He smiled broadly and turned to look at his two partners. His smile fell from his face. Jessica's and Chet's body language spoke volumes. They looked like they were preparing for their funeral. John turned back to the board for one last look through Tom's profile. He had to find the connection. He had to.

Lisa Nichols
1600 Pennsylvania Avenue

Chapter 18

First Lady Nichols rubbed her eyes as she sat back in her chair. Her office desk was covered with files. They were all on the murders of the four mourners at Captain Jason Sparks' funeral. There was knock on the door. She glanced at her watch. It was much too early for her husband to be done with briefing.

"Who is it?" She asked.

"It's Agent McDonald," the voice on the other side of the door replied. She smiled. There were already rumors that she and the agent were carrying on behind closed doors. They were carrying on, but it was not how people were thinking. There was absolutely no sexual contact between her and the agent. She was quite sure he was smitten with her, as well he should be.

Lisa Nichols was a gorgeous lady. There was no doubt that her beauty and charisma helped win her husband the election. It didn't bother Lisa; she had always known how beautiful she was. Not only had she known it, but used it to her advantage every single day of her life. Lisa smiled and called for Agent McDonald to come in.

He was carrying another manila folder, and Lisa groaned internally. She had hoped with all the red tape that had surrounded the murders and the few phone calls her people had made it would make sure this case got passed around until it was so stone cold no one could ever solve it.

"Ma'am," Agent McDonald greeted her. "Two things, first, there's good news; secondly we've had a request from the soldiers that will be attending the dinner next week." Lisa smiled.

"Well, what can I do for these men who defend our county," Lisa asked coyly.

"It seems, some of these men would like a picture with the first lady in the oval office," Agent McDonald said.

"Any chance we could 'leak' these pictures to the press?" Lisa asked.

"Oh we can do better than that, we can have this videotaped and use it as some stock footage," said Agent McDonald, smiling.

"These men are some members of the Special Forces groups, correct?" asked Lisa. Agent McDonald nodded. "Then, let's let these men come in here one at a time and have their picture made. It will get them what they want and be great publicity for us. Agent McDonald," Lisa added. "Let's don't flood this office with Secret Service while they're here. These guys don't need to feel like we don't trust them. They've protected the country for God's sake." Agent McDonald gave Lisa a withering look. Lisa smiled. "Does that cover all the dinner plans, Agent McDonald?" Luke nodded. "Then give me the good news Luke."

"The case has made its way to the FBI," Agent McDonald said. "We have suggested to our people in Washington to put Bruce Cosby on this case. We have suggested that it would make Senator Cosby very happy since this case would be a career maker." Lisa looked concerned. "You misunderstand ma'am. Bruce Cosby is an abysmal FBI agent." Lisa chuckled. "The only reason he has a job is because of who his father is. He should have the case in his hands by the end of the next week at the latest." Lisa frowned.

"Why so long?" She asked.

Agent McDonald flipped through the file. "Let's see. It is currently in the hands of a team that hasn't closed a case in three years. Huh." Lisa raised her eyebrow. Agent McDonald smiled and waved off her worry. "Oh it gets better. The team hasn't solved a case since John Fowler left them three years ago to deal with his wife's death. Rumor is he became an alcoholic while he was deep undercover, and has become a full-fledge drunk now. The two remaining agents are apparently on the verge of being reassigned. Here's where it gets really interesting. The team has pulled this guy back in as a consultant. Can you believe it?" Agent McDonald was smiling as he read off this information to Lisa. As he raised his head and saw her face, he knew trouble was brewing. Lisa looked ready to explode.

"John Fowler? The former FBI agent who helped brings down some forty plus Mafia members a few years back? That John Fowler?" Lisa was livid. Agent McDonald was nodding, but was holding his hand out trying his best to calm her.

"Ma'am, please calm down. This guy hasn't done anything in the past three years. This entire unit is on the verge of being reassigned." Lisa was anything but calm.

"AGENT MCDONALD . . ." Lisa stopped and composed herself. "Agent McDonald, do you realize that Senator Cosby has used John Fowler to make himself one of the most popular senators in the United States? Every time there is any bust that John is involved with Cosby glues himself to Fowler's side to up his approval rating. He has basically thrown his own son under the bus for this guy. John Fowler is the best there is! You do realize if Fowler hadn't left the FBI, Cosby probably would not have pulled out of the presidental race? Cosby would have won the blasted election because of his relationship with John

62

Fowler! Cosby knows he's a winner. Cosby only surrounds himself with winners!" McDonald was looking very uncomfortable and was starting to wish he was anywhere else right that moment. "Agent, let me make this very clear. 25% of John Fowler is better than 100% of most agents." Lisa stopped and drew a deep breath. She stood up, looked Agent McDonald in the face and spoke very quietly. "Get that case out of John Fowler's hands, now!" Agent McDonald ran from the room. Lisa sat back down at her desk her head in her hands.

Chapter 19

Lisa sat at her desk thinking about the newest development. She was sick to her stomach. Senator Cosby would have easily won the last election if John hadn't left the FBI. Her dreams would have been over with before they even started. The dreams she had since she was a very little girl. She wasn't President of the United States, but she was the first lady, and as far as issues she cared about, she ran the country. The people didn't need to know all of that, but the fact she knew it was enough.

She had worked so hard to make her dreams come true and now this John Fowler could come so close to derailing them; it unnerved her. She stared out the window. She was going to have to do something about Cosby. She had her best people digging into his history and the only thing she could find remotely out of place was his son being so highly ranked in the FBI. The thing is Lisa was absolutely sure that Senator Cosby had never asked a soul to move Bruce into such a place. It was just one of those things that had been done to make sure the FBI remained in Senator Cosby's favor. The strangest thing about Cosby was his relationship with John Fowler. Sure Fowler closed cases and the appearances Cosby put in with him popped Cosby's ratings, but how did Cosby find Fowler? That was a mystery for another day.

Lisa's gaze returned to the files. Cold fear gnawed at her stomach. If it was anyone else working the case, she wouldn't worry about the connections that could be made to her. But it wasn't anyone else, it was John Fowler. She shivered. It was like he was some kind of superhero. He wasn't though.

"Get a grip, girl." Lisa thought to herself. "He's just a man. He would have to know exactly where to look to even begin to unravel the web." She got up and walked over to the window. She loved the view, and tried to enjoy it. It was impossible to, however. She glanced back at the files. No, as bad as it was that John Fowler was on the case, it was even worse as to the people that had been murdered. There was the connection, the connection that she feared Fowler would figure out. Maybe it would be best if Fowler could figure it out. If someone had linked everyone else together did that mean her life was in danger? She couldn't think about it. Had someone finally figured out what had happened all those years ago? No, impossible! She noticed she was biting her fingernail. She yanked down her hand angrily. She hadn't done that in years. Not since she had known Beth.

Well there it was. Beth. She hadn't thought of her in years. She really couldn't be surprised that the memories of Beth came back to her now. Here was everyone else's picture in front of her, what could she expect? She was the only one missing from the group. Beth George . . . was this ghost finally coming back to haunt her? Tears came to Lisa's eyes. If someone saw her they would think the tears were ones of sorrow. They weren't. They were tears of fears that her life was about to come tumbling down around her and there wasn't one thing she could do to stop it.

Chapter 20

Agent McDonald sat down in his office in the security center. He was looking over all of the files he had gotten for Lisa. As he examined them he could find no connection between any of the mourners or soldier that had died.

He placed his head in his hands and thought about Lisa screaming at him. He had become enamored with "Silk". Luke had come up with that codename and the other agents all agreed. The first lady loved the name. Agent McDonald had never felt like this before in his life. Lisa was in his every thought and dream.

Agent McDonald picked up the receiver on the phone and placed a call. He had never met anyone in the group that helped the first lady with her problems. They always referred to her as Silk so there could be reasonable deniability.

"Silk would like the case we discussed earlier out of the current agent's hands." He listened to the person on the other end. "I do not know why. All I know is that is her wish." He listened for a second and responded. "Thank you." He paused. "How good a relationship do you have with Senator Cosby?" He listened for a minute. "I see. Does anyone we know have a good relationship with the senator?" McDonald listened and responded. "Okay, I will take care of it myself then." Agent McDonald hung up the phone. He got up from his desk and began to pace around his office. He wanted to make Lisa happy, but he wasn't for sure how far she wanted him to go. He walked back to his desk and decided to try the indirect approach first. He dialed the phone and waited for the voice on the other end.

"Hello, may I speak to Agent Cosby?" He listened and answered. "This is agent Luke McDonald with the Secret Service."

Vermont
John Fowler

Chapter 21

As John drove down the interstate toward the small town where Tom Bradley resided, he had to admit, Jessica knew how to take care of him. When he got off of the plane, John hadn't even thought about how to get to the Bradley residence. Jessica had reserved a car for John and had the rental company preprogram the navigation system for him. As great as that was, Jessica had made sure he had satellite radio. Eighties music was blaring out of the speakers and John was singing along at the top of his lungs.

John was smiling and thinking about life. Not two days ago, he contemplated picking up a bottle and taking a drink. Today, he didn't even think about a drink until the flight stewardess asked him if he would like something on the plane. He always thought he had been close before to breaking down and drinking. He never knew how wrong he was about that until he got on the plane.

John hated flying. When the stewardess came by with her cart, it was all John could do not to grab the entire bottle off of her cart. He settled for a soda, but he kept one eye on the cart as it went by. John gave an involuntary shudder as he thought about the flight. It wasn't that the flight was bumpy or bad, but that it was so unnatural. John shook his head and took in the countryside. He had gotten very lucky. The road had every chance of being covered in snow, but it wasn't. Snow covered the fields and trees, but the road was clear. John chuckled to himself.

John had grown up in Western Kentucky. This amount of snow would actually have been enough to close down county schools for several days. It amazed him at how little snow bothered things here. Of course there was a huge difference in the type of snow that fell in each region. Here when it snowed, it snowed. Back in Kentucky it might be freezing rain, sleet, or just flat out ice. In the northeast, the drivers here were used to driving in snow. When it snowed in Western Kentucky . . . you would think people had never seen the stuff. John was glad he didn't drive very much in New York, and he had honestly been worried about this drive in Vermont, but it had actually been very nice.

Sam, of course, had loved the snow. He thought she was slightly deranged because of it, but he had to admit New York City was beautiful at night right after a freshly fallen snow. As John looked around the countryside, he thought about how beautiful the scenery was. It looked like something right out of a Christmas card or one of those 1000 pieces puzzles Sam used to love to work on.

The GPS interrupted his thoughts. He turned onto a two lane road. Deep down he was beginning to feel dread welling up in his stomach. He always hated to talk to spouses of those that had lost loved ones, and he had no idea how he would personally react to this one. This would be the first interview he conducted since Sam's death.

As he drove down the road noticing the similarities between his former home and Vermont, he thought about his parents. He loved his parents, but he hadn't been able to face them. He thought about the look on his Mom's face when he had told her that she had raised a killer. She had known he hadn't actually killed Sam, but John had never explained to her what he had meant.

Deep down John knew he had to see his parents soon. He had to tell them what had happened, Sam would want him to. Sam loved his parents. She had always said she had wished her parents had been more like his. The one thing that John regretted the most since Sam's death was his distancing himself from them. He knew they would listen to him, tell him it wasn't his fault, but until now he wasn't ready to hear that. He didn't even know if he was now. He did know he was the closest he had been in three years to talk to them about what had happened. Once again John's GPS interrupted his thoughts.

He drove through the little town until he came upon the Bradley residence. As he pulled up in the drive, John steadied himself. He had no idea what to expect. He opened the car door and started up the walk.

Chapter 22

John walked up to the door and knocked. A couple of seconds later, the door opened.

"Mrs. Bradley?" John asked, extending his hand, "I'm John Fowler, consultant to the FBI." Mrs. Bradley shook John's hand.

"Please, call me Joan." She stepped back to let John into the house. "Welcome, and please come in." John stepped through the doorway and walked into the house. John looked around. To be a doctor's house, it was quite modest. Joan motioned for him to continue into the living room and offered him a seat. John sat down on the couch.

"Thank you for seeing me." John took a second to steady himself. "I truly mean this, I am sorry for your loss." Joan gave him a tight lip smiled and nodded for him to continue. "Joan, I need you to think real hard, do you know of any connection your husband had to the others that were murdered, or the soldier whose funeral they were attending?"

Joan looked down. John spoke very softly and encouragingly to her. "Joan, take your time. I lost my wife a few years ago, and I know how hard it is to think about your spouse in any capacity without feeling the grief." Joan squeezed John's hand, and looked up at him with tears in her eyes.

"I gave the sheriff a couple of Christmas cards that I found," replied Joan. "I have no idea when he met any of them. The other mourners I mean. He never spoke about them, and he never hung up the Christmas cards they sent. He just kept them in a box. It wasn't hidden in the attic or anything like that. It was just in a box. Everything I found I took down to the sheriff last week." John nodded and gave her an encouraging smile.

"Ok, thank you. That helps a lot. Is it ok with you if I pick those items up and take them back to New York

70

with me?" Joan nodded. "I don't want to ask you a bunch of questions that the local PD already has." Joan smiled appreciatively. "Do you mind if I look around the house and see if I can find anything that might give me a lead?"

"Mr. Fowler, you have my permission to look anywhere on my property you want." Tears glistened in Joan's eyes. "You might try his study, that's where I found the letters. I have already been through it, but you're the professional, maybe you'll find something I missed. Would you like a glass of tea?"

John smiled, "Thank you, Joan. A glass of tea would be great." Joan headed toward the kitchen and John headed toward the study. John had little hope of finding anything. He knew if Joan had been through the study and couldn't find anything, unless there were secret panels or something of that nature, he probably wouldn't have much luck. John began searching Tom's desk, bookshelf, and looked around for any hidden wall safes. After three hours of thoroughly searching the study, and three glasses of ice tea, John asked permission to take Tom's computer tower back to New York. Joan agreed. John walked back into the study and took one more look to make sure he hadn't missed anything. He couldn't help the feeling that he had missed something. As he glanced around, he realized he hadn't checked the back of the study door. He really didn't expect to find a sign with the name of the murderer, but he would take anything at this point. John closed the door to the study and looked at the back of the door.

John gave a low whistle. Now while what he found wasn't a smoking gun, it was a lead. A small one, and possibly nothing but a wild goose chase, but it was the first lead he had found in a two week old case. He walked back into the kitchen where he found Joan. She was looking through some photo albums at the kitchen table. John motioned to the seat beside her and she nodded.

71

"Joan, did you ever know of Tom living in Kentucky?"

Joan looked stunned. "Agent Fowler . . . how did you know?"

Chapter 23

John smiled inwardly at Joan's astonishment. It felt good to see one of his hunches had actually paid off. It had been so long since he had one, he had been hesitant to even broach the topic.

John had found the same familiar blue and white calendar that was hanging in John's apartment with his favorite college basketball team on the back of Tom's study door. John thought Tom was close to John's age, mid to late 30s. Now while it was possible Tom never lived in Kentucky and was enough of a fan of the Cats to hang a current basketball calendar in his personal study, John doubted it. Typically if someone was enough of a fan to hang a calendar at Tom's age, there had to be a personal connection to the team. John knew from experience if you had ever lived in Kentucky it was a tradition in many houses for one of two different college basketball calendars to hang. It was a bit of a leap in logic, but it didn't hurt to ask.

"I think he did," Joan said, looking a little ashamed. "He never talked about it, but there were things he said every now or then. Every year in March he watches college basketball and roots for the Kentucky team like it's . . ."

"A religion?" John finished the thought for her. Joan's face lit up.

"Yes!" She was very excited now. "Oh and if the games were close . . . he would pace the house like a man possessed." Her eyes were sparkling talking about Tom. John smiled inwardly. After all he had been through with Sam; he knew telling these stories about Tom were therapeutic for her.

"Was he a quiet man, or loud and boisterous . . . somewhere in between?" John asked.

"Oh he was a very quiet, patient, courteous man . . . except when basketball was on!" Joan was shaking her head and started chuckling. "One year they went into double overtime during the tournament and I thought he would have a stroke!"

John chuckled. It sounded like every Cats fan he had ever known. John needed to steer Joan to remember things she didn't know she knew.

"When do you think he was there; high school, middle school, younger?" John asked.

Joan paused for a minute. John thought he had made a mistake and Joan was about to become emotional, but after a second though she answered.

"I know he was born here in Vermont, and graduated high school in Vermont, but it seems it was sometime during his middle grades." She paused. John felt like she was about to tell him a big secret. Joan looked around like she was making sure no one was listening. She leaned in and talked softly.

"He never talked about it, but it seems like something bad happened there. Some nights he would have these dreams. He would never talk about them, but the next day he was moody, and Tom was rarely moody. One time after he got one of these Christmas cards, he had very bad dreams that night. He got up in the middle of the night and went down to his office. I came to check on him and his chair was turned away from the doorway. He was holding the letter, crying and kept saying, 'We have to tell what happened.' He sounded so distraught. I didn't want to pry you see. I love . . . loved." Joan looked up at John tears streaming down her face. John took her hands in his. "I don't know what it was all about, but Tom didn't want to share it, and Tom shared everything with me. If he didn't want me to know this, then who was I to pry?" Joan was close to breaking down. "Is this what he was killed over?"

John didn't know what to say. Joan began to sob uncontrollably.

John pulled her close and tried to console her. When she finally calmed down, she looked somewhat sheepish. "I'm sorry, Agent Fowler."

John patted her hands. "Mrs. Bradley, I don't know what happened yet, but I promise you I will do everything in my power to figure this out." Joan nodded, tears in her eyes. "Joan, I'm going to take the hard drive and the things from the sheriff's office, but I want you to know, I think you just gave me a huge lead in finding who killed your husband."

Joan smiled. John stood up and thanked her. He picked up the hard drive and headed toward his car. Joan stood on the porch watching him leave. John put the hard drive in the car and looked back toward the porch. "Mrs. Bradley," John called out. "I'm going to get who did this. I promise." Joan looked relieved. John got in the car, waved and drove off.

John never promised the victim's family that he would find the perpetrator. This time was different. He knew he would find the person responsible. He had too many people depending on him . . . but most importantly, himself.

New York FBI Office
Director Lionel Pennyworth Smothers III-Trip

Chapter 24

Trip hung up the phone. He looked very concerned. He got up from his desk and walked down the hall to Bruce's office. He hated that Bruce got all of this attention, but those in Washington had told him to offer Bruce the case. He glanced in the door and saw Bruce on the phone chatting it up. Trip thought about barging in, but knew it would be pointless. Bruce, as obnoxious as he was, never called his father about anything, and even if he did, it was not like Senator Cosby would do anything for Bruce.

Trip headed back to his office fuming. He had just been ordered to hand over the current case to Bruce and Trip had no intention of doing so. Trip knew Jessica's and Chet's careers would be doomed if he did. They wouldn't be fired, but they would never have a career that would amount to anything if he did.

Trip stormed into office and slammed the door. The more he thought about what had happened, the madder he got. He knew deep down this was some type of political maneuvering. Trip knew he had been accused by others of not sticking his neck out for his agents, but for the most part they were not in critical spots in their careers like Jessica and Chet were now. Trip sat down at his desk. He cleared his desk off. Once that was done, he leaned back in his chair, placed his feet on his desk, placed his hands together and moved them toward his face with his thumbs touching his chin and his index fingers touching his forehead. He then closed his eyes. He sat like that for nearly an hour, thinking. Suddenly he opened his eyes, removed his feet from his desk and sat forward. He had an idea. It would be a longshot, but with the situation Jessica and Chet were in, it really didn't matter. He called down to the foxhole and asked Jessica and Chet to join him in his office.

When Jessica and Chet came in, they noticed how concerned Trip looked. He shut the door and talked to them for nearly an hour. When he was done, he gave them the choice of going through with his plan, or letting Bruce have the case. Jessica and Chet were both a little stunned. Neither agent had ever heard of Trip going out of his way for agents like he was offering to. They both agreed to go along with Trip. Trip asked them if they were absolutely sure about this, because once they went down this road, there was no coming back. Chet said they had nothing left to lose, and Jessica agreed. They both watched as Trip called Bruce into Trip's office and wondered if their careers as agents were essentially over.

Chapter 25

Bruce was a little concerned about meeting with Trip. He had just received the strangest phone call from a Secret Service agent. The agent wanted to know about Bruce's relationship with his father. Bruce told the agent the truth. Bruce and his father rarely spoke. Bruce couldn't understand his father. He couldn't understand why his father wasn't more proud of him or parading him around the way he used to do with Fowler. The call didn't last very long, and if Bruce didn't know better it was almost like the Secret Service agent was vetting him for something. Bruce pushed it out of his mind as he arrived to the door of Trip's office.

Bruce knocked on Trip's door. He heard Trip shout "come in," and entered. The first thing he noticed was both Jessica and Chet seated, looking very anxious. Trip was smiling and offered Bruce a seat.

"Bruce, thanks for coming by," said Trip. "Washington has called, and they want you to take over the multiple homicide investigation that Jessica and Chet have been working on."

Bruce wasn't happy. He knew this case was cold and would be next to impossible to solve. He was thinking up several objections when Trip spoke again.

"Washington believes this is a very high profile case. Bruce, this one is probably a career maker. Of course these agents," Trip said gesturing with his hand toward Chet and Jessica. "They will both hand over any evidence they have found, plus any John may have found in his trip to Vermont." Bruce was beaming inside. He was going to take John's case away from him and the evidence.

"If that's what Washington wants, then of course I'll be glad to," said Bruce. He noticed that suddenly Jessica and Chet were both very relieved. Bruce was suddenly a little confused. He had heard through the grapevine if these

78

two didn't solve this case that they were done. The case had been snatched away from them and now they were happy. What was going on? He was even more surprised when both Jessica and Chet shook his hand and gratefully thanked him. They both asked to be excused. Bruce noticed as the two walked down the hall that they exchanged high fives. Bruce couldn't help but wonder what was going on here?

Chapter 26

Bruce watched the two walk down the hall obviously happy about the news Trip had just delivered. Did these two really care so little about their FBI careers? Bruce looked back at Trip extremely confused. Trip was busy working on files and looked up at Bruce.

"That's all I had, Bruce, if you don't mind I have a lot of paperwork here to get through," said Trip.

"Sir, may I ask you something?"

"Of course, Bruce," said Trip while shuffling through case files.

"Sir, I'm not sure how to put this so I'll just be blunt." Trip sat back, looking amused. "Sir, this was supposed to be their last case if they couldn't solve it. Those two just looked relieved. Did their careers really mean so little to them?"

Trip slowly stood up, anger building inside of him. "Bruce, they were told by Washington to give up the case. I assume they'll be given one more chance since someone went over their head. You wouldn't know anything about this would you?" Trip looked furious. "Which I really hope you do!" Trip was nearly sneering now. "Those two agents have been breaking their backs on this case and have found next to nothing, so it would serve you right if you couldn't solve it!" Bruce had his hands in front of him like he was trying to keep Trip at bay.

"Sir, I meant no disrespect. I just thought they had given up on their careers." Trip nodded and the anger left his face. "I guess the bad part is, if this is high profile, and if they were to have solved it, it would do more good for their careers than some random case they may get in the coming days."

Trip still looking slightly angry nodded. "You're exactly right. I mean they have little chance of solving it, but if they did . . . well, it doesn't matter now. I mean if you don't solve it, no one would hold it against you as cold as the case is."

Bruce saw his opportunity and sprang. "You know sir," he said trying to be sly. Trip was back to digging through files and looking away from Bruce. It was a good thing Trip wasn't looking at Bruce because it was all Trip could do to hold in his laughter. "The right thing to do would be to give them this chance." Trip looked up sharply.

"Are you telling me you want me to tell Washington you're passing on a case?" Trip asked.

"I don't want to go against my superiors, but there are times we should do what is best for the agency." Bruce was trying not to be too pleased with himself; that he may have just tied the knot in the noose around Jessica and Chet's neck.

"I guess I could tell them that you weren't comfortable taking a case away from agents that had made some progress and you have a full plate already." Trip pretended to dig around and pulled up three files that needed to be assigned. He offered them to Bruce. Bruce pressed his lips together and sighed. He knew Trip was right. He took the files and thanked Trip. Bruce turned and started out the door.

"Agent Cosby," Trip said. Bruce turned expecting to be praised for his good deed. He tried to keep the smile to himself, but failed miserably. "Shut the door on your way out." Bruce was dumbstruck. He nodded and shut the door. As he walked down the hall he looked at the three files in his hand and realized he was about to be very busy. He chuckled to himself. Why it was almost like it was busywork to keep him out of . . . no. He stopped in the hall and turned back toward Trip's door. As he reached the door he heard Trip on the phone saying that Bruce had turned down the assignment. He heard Trip say he thought it was in the best interest of the office and was proud of his agent for being a team player. Bruce started back down the hallway. He had almost embarrassed himself. To think he had almost accused his Director of something so underhanded. Bruce hurried back to his desk to start working on his new cases.

Chapter 27

Back in Trip's office, Trip was listening very carefully for the footsteps away from his door. He had been speaking to no one on the phone. Well, that was wrong; he was talking to Chet down in the foxhole. Bruce was an incompetent agent, but every now and then he did figure things out. Trip calling Chet had been Chet's idea. It seemed like a good idea, and he was very glad Chet had suggested it. Bruce would now stay out of John's, Jessica's, and Chet's hair for a little while, but they had only bought a little time.

That's what worried Trip the most. Someone somewhere had made some phone calls to arrange Bruce take this case. What worried Trip the most, if someone had done that; then they knew what kind of investigator Bruce was. Someone, very high up, was working on a cover-up. Trip shook his head. He would have to tread very carefully. This was something straight out of a conspiracy theory nut's playbook. Trip checked his watch, and decided it was time to make a phone call of his own. Trip picked up the phone and called in a favor for one of the first times in his life.

"Senator Cosby?" Trip asked. "Director Trip, of the New York FBI." He paused. "I'm doing well sir; I'm actually calling you about an old friend of yours, John Fowler." Trip listened. "Well he is back with us in a consulting position, but I think he has stumbled on something that is out of his league." Trip listened and grinned. "Yes sir, I believe he has stepped into a political landmine field, and I don't know how he managed it. Is there any way you could meet with me in my office and the three of us discuss this?" Trip listened for a minute and broke out into a full smile. "Thank you, sir. John should be here in a couple of hours. He's in Vermont now. I'll see you first thing in the morning and we'll see if we can't sort

83

this thing out." Trip listened. "Yes sir. I'll see you in the morning. Good-bye."

Trip hung up. He didn't even have to beg, which made him wonder for the thousandth time about the relationship between John Fowler and Senator Cosby. Whatever it was, it might be the only chance John, Jessica and Chet had of solving this case. Trip turned his chair and stared out the window. What had these three stumbled onto?

Chapter 28

John had been back a couple of hours, but for some reason he hadn't contacted anyone in the FBI. John realized he was following the old protocols of his team. If there was any doubt of any compromise, do not contact other team members over the phone, only face to face. He wasn't for sure why he was enacting this protocol other than his gut feeling.

This case was really starting to get to him. Five people were dead, and it appeared his home state had something to do with it. That bothered John. He had wonderful memories of Kentucky. He had grown up in western Kentucky and then went to school at Eastern Kentucky University. That was where he met the beautiful graduate student Samantha Moore. Sam was working on a Masters in Speech Pathology. Her goal was to work with children. Sam was born and raised in Virginia. Her parents, Arthur and Madeline Moore, were very, very well off. John shook his head thinking about the luxurious home they owned.

The Moore's ran in a very elite circle. It should have been no surprise to John that he would meet a one-day US senator there. Jeremiah Cosby was running for the Senate seat when John first met him. It struck him as strange that Arthur had no problems about Madeline being around Jeremiah when he first met him. Apparently Jeremiah and Madeline had just ended their relationship when Madeline met Arthur. Madeline and Arthur were together for a little over two months before they became engaged.

John soon realized that things worked a bit differently in the Moore household. Arthur was all about his business and making as many shrewd business decisions as possible. John also found that Jeremiah was the one person he had misread. John thought Jeremiah longed for Madeline, but that couldn't have been further from the truth. As John got to know Jeremiah over the years, he found out that Senator Cosby really was as squeaky clean as he appeared on TV. It was no wonder his constituents loved him.

John chuckled to himself. He had always wondered how Sam came from Madeline and Arthur. Sam would do anything for those in need, anything. She was nothing like Arthur; in fact, she was quite similar to Senator Cosby. Sam once told him she felt more of a kinship with Jeremiah than her own father. She respected Senator Cosby and truly tried to emulate him. John shook his head. Sam was more like a daughter to Senator Cosby than Bruce was a son. Sam's blue eyes would always sparkle when she talked about Senator Cosby. John used to joke with her that he was worried about losing her to him. Sam would always respond, "Eww, he's old enough to be my father."

A knock on the door pulled John away from his thoughts. He walked to the door and looked through the peep hole. Jessica was standing in the hallway. John stepped away from the peep hole. He really didn't understand what was going on inside of him. If he didn't know better, he would think he was falling for her. John looked at the picture of Sam. He took a deep breath and opened the door.

Chapter 29

"Do you always go knocking on available guy's doors late at night, Agent Hammerstein?" John asked. Jessica smiled. John felt his belly do a flip.

"Are you going to ask me in and find out, Private Investigator Fowler?" Jessica replied. John mocked a wince at the PI joke. Inside, his stomach was doing flips and flops. He stepped away from the door and gave a sweeping enter motion. Jessica smiled and walked through. John closed the door and turned around. Jessica had taken off her coat. John had always known she was attractive, but tonight for some reason she was stunning. She wasn't wearing anything provocative, or anything different than her usual FBI dress, it was like he was seeing her in a different light. John realized he hadn't breathed and had just been staring.

"Sorry, Jess . . . ah Jessica. When I fly it does funny things to me." John stammered.

"It's fine, John. Was everything all right with the car?" She asked.

John smiled a big smile, almost too big. Was he being creepy? What was wrong with him? It was like he never talked to a woman before! He had talked to Jessica thousands of times.

"I absolutely loved the satellite radio." Jessica smiled but looked a little concerned. She stepped across to him and went to feel his head to see if he had a fever. John thought she was coming to kiss him. John couldn't decide if that's what he wanted or not. In what might be the most awkward moment in the history of man and woman, John pulled his head back while puckering his lips. John realized how foolish he looked. If he didn't, the look on Jessica's face should have told him. Jessica stood in front of him. She put her hands on her hips studying John. John was turning a funny color of red. She pointed to the couch and he obediently went and sat.

"John, I am going to speak, and I want you to shut your mouth and not say a word." John nodded. "I went to feel your head because you were a funny color and your breathing seemed strange. Have you been drinking?" John shook his head no. Jessica sighed and sat down on the far end of the couch. She stared at John. She got up and sat down on the middle section beside John. She began to twirl her hair as she talked.

"John, have you been on a date since Sam died?" John looked down at the floor and shook his head no. Jessica stopped twirling her hair. She had a bemused smile on her face. She smacked his leg and John brought his head up in surprise. Jessica smiled at him.

"Let's talk business," she said. "I'm going to assume you didn't call due to old habits, which is best." John looked at her sharply. "Someone at Washington made a phone call today trying to get Bruce on the case and me and Chet off of it. Thanks to Trip, it failed." John looked completely confused. Jessica held up her hand. "It's a long story. The short of it is Senator Cosby is coming to meet with me, you, Chet, and Trip tomorrow to discuss this. For now, keep following old protocols. No calling in unless absolutely necessary." John nodded. Jessica took both of John's hands into hers. The look on her face softened. John spoke before she could.

"Jessica, I will solve this case. I'm not letting the two of you get fired, and as for that earlier . . . I'm. . ." Jessica interrupted him.

"John, I know you will. As for that other thing, you don't fly well, you're getting back out into the world for the first time in three years, and you're experiencing emotions you haven't felt during that time. You weren't for sure what I was doing, and you weren't for sure what you

88

wanted me to do. It's ok, I understand." She smiled at him warmly, and John felt his stomach flip again. Then Jessica leaned in very slowly. Not to kiss him but John thought to whisper into his ear. John's heart was racing. Jessica whispered in his ear.

"John, have no fear, if I was coming on to you, you would know it." Jessica leaned back, smiled, and straightened the collar of his shirt. John swallowed. Jessica stood up and headed for the door.

"Don't get up," she said. "I'll show myself out. I'll see you in the morning."

John watched the door shut and sat there for several minutes. He leaned back on the couch.

"Sam, I know you're laughing at me right now." John listened to the silence, not expecting an answer, but listening just the same. "I love you, Sam, but I've got to live my life. I hope you understand." John leaned forward and put his head in his hands. He used to sit this way at home when a case would bother him, and Sam would put her arms around his shoulders. He swore he could feel them around him right now.

Chapter 30

John arrived at 9:00 the next morning at the NY FBI Building. As John entered the foxhole, he chuckled at the irony. If Bruce knew who was down here he would quite possibly explode. John looked across the room and saw Jessica leaning against the desk along the far wall. From her vantage point she could see who was entering. John could see the amusement on her face. For some reason John pictured a cat playing with a mouse before the cat killed the mouse. John was pretty sure he was the mouse in that scenario.

He tore his eyes off of Jessica and looked around the room. There was Chet, Trip, and of course the US senator himself, Jeremiah Cosby. Trip saw John and motioned him over. Trip gave an account of what had happened the day before with Bruce and Washington so John would be up to speed.

"Senator, do you have any clue what is going on here?" John asked after Trip had finished.

"John, I have no idea what is going on, but I can tell you one thing. You've stepped in it. I'm not for sure what it is, but it stinks high to heaven." Senator Cosby replied.

John loved talking with Senator Cosby. He had the look of a distinguished Virginian and he spoke with an accent that just made John feel at home. Senator Cosby also told it like it was. It was refreshing to talk to him about anything. John felt dirty to even have to ask the following question.

John started to speak, "Uh, senator, I have to ask . . ."

Senator Cosby interrupted. "Ma'boy, you wouldn't be who you are if you didn't ask, but let me assure you I would rather chew my own leg off than call and ask a favor for that good-for-nothing son of mine. No, John. I have nothing to do with this mess you've stumbled into." The senator smiled warmly at John.

"I apologize for even having to ask it, sir," said John.

"Think nothing of it, ma'boy. I would say you're on the right thinking track. It would take someone with my standing or higher to pull those strings. I shudder to think how far up the chain you might have to pull, if you get my drift."

John did get his drift. There would be no paper trail to follow this one on either. This was put in play with backroom nudges and handshakes on golf courses stuff . . . the kind of stuff that John was terrible at. Someone with an awful lot of stroke had something to do with this.

"John," the senator said. "I'm going to have my most trusted people keep their ear on the ground. I doubt they'll hear anything worth telling, but who knows what someone, somewhere might say. I hate to dash, but I do have some meetings I need to attend, and I would like to have a private word with you if that's all right?" John nodded and they walked out of the foxhole.

Chapter 31

Outside of the foxhole, Senator Cosby looked John up and down, as if trying to decide what to say.

"Sen . . . Jeremiah, we've known each other too long. Say what you have to say. Chances are I deserve it," said John.

"All right then, ma'boy," began the senator. "First, I'm glad to see you back on your feet. You're too good of an agent to be one of those private investigators." John braced himself. If Jeremiah was going to butter him up, then there was a doozy of a criticism coming.

Jeremiah looked John right in the eye. "Boy, you've got some nerve with some of the things you said to Arthur and Madeline!"

John couldn't help himself, "Would that be the part where I said to them the only reason both of your eyes are brown is that you're both full of crap?"

Jeremiah nearly exploded. "Tarnation son! Now I'll admit Arthur is about the biggest curmudgeon the world has ever seen, but that is no way to treat Madeline! Furthermore, why haven't you opened up the case file on Sam?"

John looked down, ashamed. He looked back up with tears in his eyes, and Jeremiah's face softened. Jeremiah spoke, his voice much softer.

"Now, now son, you have to ignore this old fool sometimes. I know why you haven't opened the case . . . you're not ready are you?" John nodded. Jeremiah looked at him with a slow smile coming to his face. "I guess I'm maddest at you for telling off Arthur and me not seeing it."

John had a choked laugh. Jeremiah went on. "I bet he drew up like a big ole bull; his nostrils flaring in and out." Jeremiah chuckled and continued. "That good- for- nothing pompous windbag." Now John was having a full-on laughing fit. Jeremiah joined in. After a second they stopped, and Jeremiah hugged John. Jeremiah stepped back and stuck his finger in John's chest.

"Boy, it's alright to miss her, but you have to live. You and I both know Sam wouldn't want you carrying on like this. Now, what about that Jessica in there? I think she's got it bad for you." John smiled and so did Jeremiah.

"I'm sorry, Jeremiah. I should have called you, but you reminded me of Sam too much." Jeremiah nodded. "Jeremiah, she thought of you as a father, you know that right?" Jeremiah's eyes were moist with forming tears.

"I thought of her as a daughter, but more importantly I think of you as the son I never had," Jeremiah stated. John roared with laughter, and Jeremiah joined in. "Now do me a favor, come upstairs and shake my hand in the hallway in front of his office so he'll be mad for the next several days. That should buy you some more time." John laughed, and clapped Jeremiah on the back as they headed to the elevator.

Chapter 32

Bruce watched out of the glass window to his office as his father and John shook hands. Bruce drank his coffee and chuckled to himself. He didn't know which man he hated worse, John for trying to replace him as his father's son, or his father for trying to replace his son. The old man had no idea what all Bruce had done for him.

Bruce knew he wasn't as good as a detective as John Fowler, but Bruce wasn't as dumb as he let on. There was obviously something huge going on with the current case John was working on. Fine, let him have it. Bruce really could care less. He wanted to see John and his group of merry men booted out of the FBI, but Bruce knew you can't always get what you want. As long as John was busy on this case, that kept him away from the murder case of his wife. Bruce didn't think he could take John crying and moaning about his dead wife any longer.

Bruce smiled at John as his father left the building. Bruce's mind was in motion. Bruce chuckled to himself, proud of how he had outfoxed John, his father, and the entire FBI. The best part was they had no idea.

Chapter 33

As John headed downstairs a cold shiver came over him. He assumed it was from seeing Bruce smile. John had never seen a snake smile before, but he was quite confident if one did it would resemble the smile Bruce just gave him. John had a nagging feeling that their conflict was going to come to a head, sooner rather than later.

As John stepped off the elevator and looked down toward the foxhole, he could hear the voices of his team and Trip. None of them sounded too confident. John smiled to himself. That would all change in just a moment when he told them what he had found and let the mad web surfer Chet do his thing.

"So does anyone want to know what I found out in Vermont?" John asked as he entered the room. Jessica's eyebrows lifted up.

"You actually found something?" She asked in amazement. "What could you have possibly found there?" John pointed to the hard drive of the computer he had brought back from Vermont. Chet looked very happy.

"Not yet my friend," John said, wagging his finger back in forth in the air. "While you might find something interesting in that computer, I think the thing you'll find most interesting is that the good Doctor Bradley did not live his entire life in Vermont." This revelation got Trip's attention. He had been leaning against a desk to the left of John with his arms folded. When John informed them of the new lead Trip unfolded his arms and turned toward John.

"Where did he live besides Vermont?" Trip asked.

"It seems he lived in Kentucky for a few years. Apparently he lived there sometime during his middle grade years," John replied. With that information, Chet began to work his fingers on the computers. Chet started pulling up files left and right. He did look disappointed however.

"I got some of this information yesterday boss, and entered it all digitally. The problem is none of these kids lived in the same town, most of them went to different county schools." Chet replied. He turned to look at John. John was looking at the screen. Something was bothering him. John looked closely at the name of the different counties. Something clicked in John's head and his demeanor changed. Chet was confused by the small smirk that was growing across John's face.

"Chet, I'm assuming you have the ability to pull up a county map of Kentucky and shade in the counties in which each middle school the victims attended is located in?" John asked. Chet gave him a look like John had insulted his intelligence.

"Sorry, Chet." Chet shrugged it off. A map pulled up of the state. The counties were starting to highlight on the map. The four counties that were highlighting were all touching. Jessica and Trip both walked forward in amazement while John chuckled. John had found the connection where no one else could. He put his hands in his pants pockets and rocked back on his heels. It was something John used to do when he had cracked, or just solved, a case. He had done it.

Chapter 34

"Did you know?" Jessica asked. John shrugged his shoulders; Jessica slapped his arm with the back of her hand. "HOW?"

John had a broad grin on his face. Jessica looked like she could slap John. He ignored her for a minute, and walked back to Chet.

"Now if you can, enlarge the map, and if you could keep on there any churches, oh, and if you can highlight the addresses of the victims, and locate what would have been the biggest plant or factory in the area. Once you do that, see if it has offices in Tennessee, Vermont, Illinois, and . . ."

"Florida," Jessica said interrupting him. "Of course, of course!" She whacked John on his shoulder again. "Why else would these people move in and go back to where they came from!" Trip looked all kinds of confused.

"Will someone please explain what in the Sam Hill is going on?" Trip asked. John looked at Jessica and waved her on.

"I don't understand it all myself yet, sir, but my guess is these folks' parents worked for some factory or company that was based in the victim's home states," Jessica began.

"Archibald Industries!" Chet exclaimed. "In 1984, Archibald Industries opened a plant in Kentucky and, it seems, brought in people from other plants to work in administration. Yep, that was the last one sir, all of these victims who moved back to their home states worked for Archibald. Apparently they went back home after a few years."

Trip still looked confused, Jessica started to talk, but Trip held up his hand. He turned toward John. Trip pointed his finger in John's chest. "Stop smiling, and tell me how? How did you know?"

John smirked and quickly wiped it from his face when Trip's irritation level went even higher.

"Well, sir, Tom Bradley had a Cats' calendar . . . the college basketball team, sir?" Trip nodded very slowly, John continued. "He had one in his house so I simply asked his wife if he ever lived in Kentucky. When she said she thought he had, I managed to contact the high school he graduated from and got his transfer information. I contacted that school and found out no one else had gone there. The secretary did go on to say that was about the time the new plant opened and people that had moved in had a hard time finding housing already available in the county."

Jessica snapped her fingers, "Of course! So they moved somewhere nearby and their children went to the county schools of the county they lived in."

Chet looked bewildered. "County schools?"

Jessica smiled. "Oh did you fall asleep during our esteemed colleague's tales of his home state?" Chet looked a bit sheepish. "How many counties are in Kentucky, John?"

"120 I do believe," began John.

"So they all moved as close as they could to the plant," interrupted Trip. He walked toward the screen. "And after their time was up at the plant or however they worked it out, they went back to their home states. Captain Jason Sparks was born in the county where the plant was located, so that explains his connection." Trip walked away deep in thought. He was rubbing his forehead with his forefinger and his thumb. He stopped walking and a smile came to his face. He turned around and walked up to John. Trip looked quite pleased with himself. He looked John up and down, a bit smugly.

John and Trip had quite an interesting relationship. John was good and he knew it. When Trip needed something solved, he always gave it to John. Trip just wished John didn't know he was so good. So whenever the opportunity presented itself for Trip to knock John down a peg or two, Trip relished the idea. Jessica was watching the whole exchange, smiling inwardly. This was the John and Trip of old, something she had so desperately wanted to see again . . . for John's sake.

Trip looked John right in the eye, and asked him the question that he was sure would deflate John's ego. "Where did they meet?" Trip asked very quietly.

"Well, I'm not sure," began John. Trip smiled smugly and began to nod his head. John continued. "But if you made me guess, since they're all roughly the same age, I would say it would be church." Trip looked a little confused.

"Sir," John began, "Kentucky is part of the Bible belt. If you're an outsider and you want to fit in, especially if you're coming in from the outside to start up a factory that you need the locals to run, you had best be in church. In this area, when someone is sick, has a child, loses a relative, or something like that, the church will make meals, help with childcare, or whatever a person needs." John looked around the room, noticing everyone was still with him. He continued.

"The church is a vital part of the community there. Not just for religious reasons. Sunday school classes have meetings all over town. In some of the larger cities, a group of men will meet at a restaurant on a certain morning each week and have a Bible class, but not just teaching and learning is experienced. You also have a fellowship and kinship with each other. If you are going to be a part of this small community and you want to really be ingrained, then you need to be in a church. My guess is, if the owner of the plant had anything to do about it, he sent them to a certain church. That could be wrong, but I'm guessing if you send me and my team to Kentucky we will find this church and the connection."

John was rocking again. Trip was impressed. Three years away, a stone cold dead case, and John had found the lead. Trip really hated the words that came out of his mouth.

"No, your team is not going to Kentucky."

Chapter 35

John looked like he had been punched in the stomach. He started to walk out of the room. Trip stopped him.

"John, wait, you don't understand. I can't authorize all of you to go to Kentucky. Someone in Washington will find out." John quickly understood.

If this case was being watched by those on high, then the authorization of all three to go to Kentucky would stand out. John had an idea. He wasn't crazy about it, but he knew it was their only shot.

"Sir, I could go. The case is dead, I'm done with it, and I could fly home to see my folks. I might make a slight detour, and if I should stumble across some information, then is it possible the FBI could reimburse me?"

Trip's smile lit up the entire room.

"John, did I tell you I missed you being around?" Trip clapped John on the back. "Great work, Agent." John looked at Trip to make sure he hadn't misheard. The look on Trip's face let him know he hadn't. John sighed. Jessica walked over and put her hand on John's shoulder to make sure he was okay. John normally would have said he was fine and pulled away. Today, he looked over his shoulder at her, and patted her hand on his shoulder. Trip motioned to Chet to leave the room with him. Jessica and John never noticed.

Outside the room, Trip turned to Chet.

"How long has that been brewing?" Trip asked.

"Honestly, for ten years now," Chet replied. Trip looked shocked. "You misunderstand sir; they would never, ever admit they had feelings for each other when Sam was alive. There was never a chance either of them would do anything to hurt Sam. I'll tell you something even the great John Fowler doesn't know." Trip looked very interested. "Jessica was very close with Sam. Jessica

101

would call Sam often and let her know what was going on with John. In fact, they had lunch at least once a week together."

Trip nodded. "I knew that." Chet was surprised. Trip pointed his finger at John and Jessica. "So are they . . ."

"NO, SIR!" Trip jumped back. "I'm sorry, sir!" Chet stammered. "It's just those two . . . you know I tried to date her." Trip nodded. "It was the worst mistake of my life. She only has eyes for him. She keeps saying she'll find someone someday. She's found him, sir, and she's not going to let him get away, but she would never do anything inappropriate."

Trip nodded, "I imagine with everything John's gone through with Sam he's got the game of a 14-year old?" Chet winced, but nodded. Trip sighed. "If he comes back, it's going to be weird around here isn't it?" Chet nodded again. "Are you okay with them . . . well whatever it is they're doing?" Once again Chet nodded. Trip sighed and straightened. "Then I'll guess we'll let them do whatever it is they're going to do. God knows John can't afford any more setbacks right now." Chet nodded. "To tell you the truth, Chet, I kind of think they deserve each other."

Chapter 36

Trip peeked back into the foxhole. Jessica and John were looking on the computer at flights to Kentucky. They were standing very near each other. John's left hand was less than an inch from Jessica's right hand. Several times they brushed each other, but they never touched. As Trip started to pull away, he noticed Jessica stop looking at the screen and was looking directly at John. Then Jessica would begin to look at the screen and John would stare at her.

Trip turned and walked away. This was going to be like a bad romance movie for a long time. Trip and Chet walked to the elevator and headed upstairs.

When Jessica heard the elevator doors close, she took her right hand and slid it on top of John's left. John froze. He swallowed audibly. Jessica was trying to keep a straight face but was failing miserably. John turned and looked at her. He swallowed and spoke.

"Jessica, I have a confession to make. I've only dated one person in my entire life." Jessica's eyes widened with surprise. She started to speak, stopped, started again, and then stopped.

"Wait . . . wait . . . you, Mr. I know-how-good-I-look, Mr. I-can-solve-any-crime-and-look-good-in-my-hat-doing-it?"

"You like my hat?" John interrupted.

She continued, ignoring his comment. "Mr. I-know-I'm-fine-as-wine? YOU?" Jessica was flabbergasted. "Are you telling me you've only dated one person in your entire life or are you saying . . . "

Jessica left the question hanging in the air. He held up one finger. His face was beat red. Jessica held her hands to her face trying to hold back the astonishment.

"John, wow, ok, look. First of all, there is absolutely nothing wrong with that. In fact, it's rather

103

honorable, but the big game you use to talk . . ." John kept looking at the floor not saying a word. She walked over to him, crooked her finger, and used it to raise his chin until he was looking her in the eyes. "John . . . We will take this . . . whatever this is . . . as slow as you need to. I have no idea where your mind, heart, or anything else is right now."

John nodded. He leaned forward and kissed her forehead. He brushed the hair out of her face. Jessica had forgotten to breathe. As he turned and walked away she almost gasped. She steadied herself. She called after him.

"John." He turned around. He looked at her, deep in her eyes. Jessica had never seen him look like that at her before. Her legs went a little weak and she put out a hand on the desk to steady herself. She would have run to him, but she really couldn't move. She lost her words. He tipped his hat and sauntered out the door, smiling to himself. It took a second for Jessica to steady herself after he left.

"Wow!" That was all she could say.

Interlude
David George

Chapter 37

David George looked at himself in the mirror. He was wearing his military dress uniform. He was proud to serve his country; he only wished those in that office felt the same. He hated that those that served pretended to be something they weren't. Actually, there was only one person he actually knew that was true of.

David looked down at the letter he had received. He and three other soldiers had been cleared to have their picture made with the first lady in the Oval office. David had hoped it would not come to this, but he would carry out his mission, no matter what it took. He owed Beth that. David shook his head. Things weren't going the way he planned.

He truly believed the note he left on the bodies at the funeral of Jason would have brought out the truth, but it didn't and David only had one choice left. He wasn't about to just kill Veronica. No, she had to tell what happened. She had to tell everything; every gory detail. She had to tell how it was her fault that Beth was dead and if it had been up to Veronica, he would have been as well.

The memories started to come back to him again. He thought of the small town where he grew up in Kentucky. When Veronica and the other kids showed up, everyone ignored Beth and David, except Veronica. In fact, it was almost like when Veronica found out how bad he and Beth had it, Veronica became more involved in their lives. David had to admit, for a while Veronica did make their lives better.

David never trusted Veronica. He was sure it started out mostly because he thought she was trying to steal Beth from him. There was more than that though. There was something manipulating and calculating about Veronica. She always had to have everything her way. It was bad enough to watch her run over everyone at church, but when David overheard Beth talking to Brother Jim . . . David knew Brother Jim was right, Veronica couldn't be trusted with Beth's secret. Not because Veronica cared about Beth; no, that wasn't it at all. The truth was Beth's secret would affect Veronica. It was all about Veronica. It was always all about Veronica.

David looked down at the invitation to the White House. It was all about Veronica, and David couldn't wait until she got the justice she deserved. In three days, David would be in the White House and he would get her to confess everything . . . and if she wouldn't . . . David just smiled.

John Fowler
Kentucky

Chapter 38

It was Sunday morning, and John's plane had landed a few hours earlier. Once again Jessica had rented him a car complete with satellite radio. The 80's channel was blaring again, and John was singing along at the top of his lungs. John was trying to keep his mind off the fact he was less than 200 miles away from his parents' farm. He was doing a pretty pitiful job of it, truth be told. He was in Kentucky, and all he could think about was going home.

His GPS went off, and John turned off the interstate. He had about a 45 minute drive in front of him on two lanes, or less, roads. John looked over the car and thought about how grateful he was for Jessica providing it for him. Then his mind drifted to Jessica. He shook his head. What a hot mess he became when she was around. He knew what he wanted to do, but was that fair? Was it fair to Sam? He looked over in the passenger seat and saw Sam.

John looked back at the road and then his brain just processed what he saw. He looked back. There she was, real. She wasn't some transparent apparition or ghost. It was Sam! John stopped in midsentence of the song he was singing.

"You know I do not understand why you say this is our song. You were born in Kentucky. I just think you liked to sing that song to me any chance you got," she said. John's mouth was open. He stared at the road, jerked the wheel and then straightened the car and looked back.

"I'm still here," she said.

John pinched himself three times and kept looking over at the passenger seat. Sam waved.

"You know for a world class detective, you're an idiot," she said smiling. Sam was smiling the million watt smile that had won John's heart. All John could think about was how he missed her. She was so beautiful. "Now don't start crying or you'll wreck the car and kill yourself," she scolded. John nodded.

"Mister Detective, think. Is this really me?" She chided.

John looked at her. She was solid, at least she looked solid. He reached out to touch her, but stopped. He was afraid if he went down that road he could be looking at a stay at the funny farm.

"Ok, if you were a ghost," John began. Sam gave him a withering look. Sam was an absolute skeptic, which had some irony given the current situation. He continued, "If you were a ghost, the chances of you being here, solid-looking for this long are minute from everything I've read. And besides, you always swore you wouldn't haunt me." Sam smiled. "No, this is most likely my subconscious telling me you and I need to have a conversation." Sam looked bemused.

"You mean about the fact that you keep saying it's not fair of you to not move on with your life after three years?" Sam asked. "Or, one of my favorites, how it's your fault I'm dead? Last time I checked, Sweetie, you didn't set the bomb that blew up the apartment and you were over a block away from the apartment when it blew. Or wait, this one is definitely my favorite; every time you get close to Jessica you back off, because you're afraid of losing someone in a relationship and blame it on your lack of," Sam used air quotes, "'game'?"

John spun in the seat, shocked. "Are you trying to say that I have commitment issues because of what happened to you?"

"You're subconscious is the one saying that, not me, remember? What I would say is that you are scared. What I'm also saying is someone is having issues if the first time you see your dead wife is three years after she died. Although, I have to admit you did a fine job wallowing in self-pity those three years. You should have gotten some kind of award for that."

"You think I'm using you as a way to stay away from Jessica?" John asked.

"I think it's time to admit you're alone in this car arguing with yourself. That's the kind of thing that will get you a trip to the little room with the suit that lets you hug yourself." Sam looked John right into his eyes. "It's time to live, John."

Tears welled in John's eyes. "I miss you, Sam." John's voice cracked.

"Well if you don't pay attention to the road, you're going to see me a lot sooner than you expected," said Sam.

John whipped around to watch the road. When he turned back to Sam, she was gone. John flipped the dial around on the radio trying out different current music stations. After about five minutes of no luck, he settled on an oldies station. John found a band singing one of his favorites.

"Ok, time to move on with my life, but crazy subconscious or no, I'm still listening to my music," John said out loud. He swore he heard Sam say, "I wouldn't expect anything less."

Chapter 39

As John pulled into the little sleepy town where Archibald Industries was located, he was reminded of his hometown around this time on Sunday mornings. Some stores were open, but there were very few people out. John pulled into the parking lot of Archibald Industries. Down the street he saw a huge house with no cars to be seen, and no signs of life. There was a for sale sign in the yard that appeared to have been there for many years. The house was very out of place. It was much too large compared to the other houses and shops. John was sure that was where the owner of Archibald Industries used to live.

John was certain he had found the epicenter of this case. Somewhere in this little town was the cause of what led to the quadruple homicide he was investigating. John looked around and noticed someone walking around the grounds of the big house. John jumped into his car and drove over to try and talk to the man.

As John pulled up the drive, the man walked over to him.

"You interested in buying the place?" He asked.

"No, sir, I am working with the FBI on a case, and wondered if you could answer a few questions," said John. The man looked around to see if anyone was watching. The caretaker looked very distrusting of John.

"Look, I only have one real question. The man who owned this house, was there a particular church that he attended?" John asked. The man brightened right up, and then started to look a little nervous.

"Yes, sir, he did. Um, would you mind not telling anyone there you saw me today? I needed to get a few things done . . ." John interrupted him.

"You have nothing to fear; in fact I don't even know your name. NO! Don't tell me!" John had to stop the caretaker before he blurted it out. "All I want to know is where is the church and what is its name?"

"That's easy. He attended Double Forks Southern Missionary Baptist Church," the caretaker replied. John nodded. The caretaker gave him the directions and John thanked him. John drove over to the church, found an empty parking spot, parked his car and looked around. The lot was full, and the large bell on top of the steeple had just finished ringing. John stood and was surprised how much it reminded him of home. As he stood there, he listened to the music that came out of the church. The congregation had begun singing a familiar hymn, in fact it had been his mother's favorite when he was growing up.

John hesitated. He hadn't been to church in three years. As he stood there trying to muster the strength to walk into the doors, he could hear his mother. It was the day of Sam's funeral and the last time they had talked.

"Not only should you go to church," John remembered her saying, "but it would do you some good. God didn't fail you, John. What happened, it happened for a reason. God didn't make that person blow up your apartment. You don't blame God for an evil man doing evil things. Did God stop whoever from blowing it up? No. But there's a reason it all happened, John, and you need to accept that before you can move forward. Sam would want you to move forward, John. You need to believe that."

John had to agree with her. Man, in one day he had seen his late wife, and remembered the last discussion he had with his mother. He didn't know how much more of these trips down memory lane he could take. John smiled and opened the door to the church. He heard the lyrics as he walked through the door. "I once was lost, but now I'm found, was blind, but now I see."

111

Brother Jim
Pastor of Double Forks Southern Missionary
Baptist Church

Chapter 40

Brother Jim noticed the man walk in dressed in only what he could call a FBI suit. As the congregation was singing, Jim realized the moment he had been waiting for had finally come. For over twenty-five years Brother Jim kept waiting for someone to question him. He knew this day had been coming, but for some reason instead of fear, he felt relief.

The past few weeks he had been jumping every time the phone rang, or a strange car drove through town. Ever since Brother Jim had read about the death of Captain Jason Sparks and then the quadruple murders, he knew it was a matter of time before someone came to ask him some questions.

Brother Jim had been with the church for over forty years. He knew some preachers left and went to serve at another church but he had never felt the Lord lead him anywhere else. In fact, ever since Beth and David George disappeared, he knew he wouldn't be leaving this church until this day came.

The service continued as normal. Brother Jim watched the FBI agent. To Brother Jim's surprise, the agent sang the songs, and honestly seemed to feel as at home as someone could be while visiting a church.

When Brother Jim stood up to preach, he laughed to himself the irony of the days message, God's forgiveness. Brother Jim knew in his heart he did nothing wrong, but he still had regret. He had regret that he hadn't done more.

He had no proof what happened that day; just what he suspected. Brother Jim smiled, and stepped to the podium.

"Brothers and Sisters, let me welcome you to the Lord's house," he paused waiting for the scattering of Amens. "I have an announcement to make before I begin. Tonight, there will be no service. Tonight, I would like you to check on those in this town that are less fortunate than others, perhaps have a group meal. Tonight, we need to take care of those who need our help. We need to take care of those who don't have the ability to do for themselves what needs to be done. Now if you will open your Bible. . ." Brother Jim began to preach. After the message was over, he went to the back of the church as always and shook hands with each person that walked out until the only person left was the FBI agent. Brother Jim smiled; he was ready to lift the burden he had been carrying all of these years off of his shoulders.

John Fowler
Double Forks Southern Missionary Baptist
Church

Chapter 41

As John sat in the service and listened to the preacher, he thought about how everyone had been addressing each other. At most places, it was Reverend so and so, or Pastor so and so, but not here, and not at John's home church. Where he grew up, it was Brother so and so, and Sister so and so. He saw this church was exactly the same as the one he grew up in. As the preacher spoke, John wondered if this was a wild goose chase that would lead to a dead end. Whatever happened in this town, it had happened over twenty-five years ago. He knew it was possible this was the same preacher, but it was also very possible it wasn't.

As the service ended, John tried to stay in the back of the crowd to make sure he was the last one to go through the door. It was very hard. Many of the members had come up to him and were shaking his hand and inviting him for a meal that afternoon or evening. John politely declined them all explaining he would probably be heading toward his parents' home. John wondered what had brought out that answer. He looked around the church and he knew. This place so reminded him of home. Maybe if he could get everything cleared up today, John would go visit his parents.

As the last member of the congregation left, John stepped through the door. The preacher reached out his hand and spoke.

"FBI?" Brother Jim asked. John was taken aback for a second and looked down at his suit. There was a certain something about it that screamed "G-Man". John nodded.

"Sir, I have a question about some children that would have lived here over twenty-five years ago," said John.

"Let's walk outside. There are some things that don't need to be talked about inside a church. While there are many bad things that are discussed in the Bible, what happened in this town isn't one of those things I want to talk about in this building." Brother Jim led John outside. John thought he was finally on the right track. Had he finally stumbled on, in this little town, what had led to all of these murders? More importantly, how did the preacher fit in? John followed, anxious for the answers.

Chapter 42

It was warm for February. John and the preacher sat down on the steps of the porch of the church. John extended his hand to the preacher. Brother Jim looked a little confused.

"I'm John, John Fowler. If I'm going to question someone, you need to know my name." Brother Jim smiled and shook John's hand. Brother Jim stood up and looked out to the wooded areas around the church.

"Agent Fowler," Brother Jim began. John interrupted him.

"John. Just John."

"Fair enough, John," Brother Jim said smiling. "Can I ask you specifically why you're here?"

"I'm here about the deaths of five different people: Jason Sparks, Tom Bradley, Amy Jensen, Leroy Jenkins, and Colt McCormick. All of these individuals grew up in this general vicinity. Excuse me, let me correct myself, four of them may have moved here and then moved away later in their youth." John was looking the preacher in his eyes. The preacher dropped John's gaze and looked down at the ground. Brother Jim smiled as he looked back at John.

"John, you're wrong. I've been waiting for you, sir. I've been waiting for you for over two decades." John was astonished at the preacher's revelation.

"I'm wrong?" John asked. "Sir, not to be rude, but I have five bodies that say otherwise."

"John, if I'm right about what happened, you have six bodies, and if this goes the way I think it will, you'll have seven before this is over with. You've stumbled onto something that has been brewing for over twenty five years. You've stumbled onto what some would call a conspiracy. I wouldn't. I simply call it like I see it. You have stumbled upon the biggest spoiled brat getting exactly what she

116

wanted no matter how many innocent people had to die for her to get it!" John was confused. He didn't know what to think, but he wasn't leaving this preacher or town, until he had the answers he wanted. If he had to, he was prepared to arrest Brother Jim and bring him back with him. The preacher looked very old suddenly. It was obvious to John that whatever had happened here, it had bothered Brother Jim for a very long time. The guilt on the preacher's face was heartbreaking. John wanted to feel for the man, but he couldn't. Not yet. Not until he knew what had happened here that caused five deaths. Brother Jim continued.

"I don't know much, sir, but I will tell you everything I do know. All I ask is you understand something. I am a man, and a man makes mistakes. I have regretted the mistake I made all those years ago and every day after it." Jim felt a burden starting to lift of his chest. "I'm sorry. I'm speaking in riddles. Let me tell you what I know happened, and then if you're interested I'll tell you what I think happened after that."

Chapter 43

John leaned back against the pillars on the porch and listened. Brother Jim fought back the tears in his eyes. He sighed and began.

"You have to understand, first, the time that we are talking about. I think the plant came into the community in '82 or '83. There wasn't much here, John. Mostly farmers and a few miners were still here. The majority of the mines had shut down by this time. There was so little down there and the accidents . . . well, it just wasn't worth it."

"When Mr. Staples approached the town about building here, it was . . . well it was like answered prayers. We let him have all sorts of tax breaks. We just needed to have the jobs. We understood it was mostly the manual labor jobs, at first, the townsfolk could apply for. It didn't matter. I don't know how much you remember about that time, but people were seeing 18% interest rates on their homes. It was a bad time, John, and sometimes in bad times, you don't look too hard when someone offers you a gift."

Jim looked at John, "I don't want to sound like I'm not grateful to the man, and no matter how hard we dug, we never would have known about his daughter . . . Veronica. You know how there are some people out there that think the sun was made to shine on them? Well, whoever they are, they are saints compared to Veronica Staples."

John was confused about the whole conversation. The name Veronica was gnawing at him. It finally dawned on him, the note the killer left, "Tell Veronica she's next." John's mind was racing trying to put together pieces of the puzzle. He looked at Brother Jim; John's eyes were dancing. Jim paused his story after noticing John was trying to figure things out.

"Brother Jim, you've just mentioned a name that is connected to this case that hasn't been in any of the

118

papers." Jim sighed, and looked at the ground. When he brought his head back up he looked remorseful.

"I was afraid of that. Let me continue and you'll understand soon." John nodded and Jim continued.

"When Veronica first showed up, she seemed to be the sweetest angel, and then I overheard some kids talking about her one day. They all said the same thing; when no adults were around, she treated everyone like dirt. Now, that's nothing new in that age of a child, but when I one day witnessed it . . . John, it was like she thought some of these children should worship her. But I'm skipping ahead, let me back up."

"Some people were brought in from other plants, and of course they brought their children with them. These children, Veronica and two of the local children were in the same Sunday school class together. Tom Bradley, Amy Jensen, Leroy Jenkins, Colt McCormick, Veronica Nichols, local kid Jason Sparks, and another local kid whose name you haven't heard yet if I have my guess, Beth George."

Now John had two names that he didn't have before this trip. John felt there was more. He waited. Brother Jim wasn't going to quit now. Not when he had so much guilt welled up inside. Brother Jim gathered his thoughts and continued.

"For the next oh, five or six years, they were inseparable. Sure they attended different schools, but in the summer, they went everywhere together, and they had a tag along, Beth's little brother, David George. Another name I'm sure you don't have yet."

Brother Jim stopped. John waited. John saw the tears starting to flow down Jim's cheeks.

"John, it's my fault. I knew. I knew and I could have stopped it. It's the same as if I pulled the trigger to kill all of them myself." John sat on the porch watching the preacher break down and sob uncontrollably, understanding exactly how the man felt.

Chapter 44

Brother Jim sobbed for a few minutes. John sat lost in his thoughts. Here was a man of God blaming himself for all five deaths, and unless John had completely lost his detective skills, Jim had nothing to do with the actual deaths. The irony was not lost on John.

"Sorry, John," said the pastor.

"Think nothing of it. You know, Brother Jim, I lost my wife three years ago. She was killed when a bomb went off in my apartment that I can only assume was meant for me."

Brother Jim sat up straight, "You're that John Fowler? The one I saw them talking about on the news for, like, two weeks?" John nodded. "I should have known there weren't that many agents with that name. It shouldn't surprise me that you are the one here today asking me questions." Brother Jim paused, and looked at John strangely. He went ahead with his question, timidly. "Aren't you supposed to be dead?"

John laughed. "Well, we let the Mafia think that. My Mom told me something after the funeral it has taken me three years to even begin to get through my head. She basically said it wasn't my fault someone did something evil, it wasn't God's fault that he allowed something evil to happen, it's the person's fault that committed the act."

Brother Jim smiled. "You have a very wise mother John. It's always easier to give that advice than to accept it, I have found over the years." He paused. "I'm ready to tell you the rest, if you're ready to listen." John nodded.

"Veronica took to Beth and David George immediately. When I look back at it now, it was almost like she was practicing to help out those less fortunate and putting it on her resume. John, I promise you, this girl has been practicing to be the most powerful woman in the United States since birth. And have no fear; she will do whatever it takes to be that person. Do you understand what I am saying? Whatever it takes! Veronica did the right things for all the wrong reasons. She wanted the glory and notice when she did something. Do you understand what I mean?"

John nodded but didn't quite understand what the preacher was getting at. Something still didn't sit right with John. If this girl was out to be the most powerful woman in the US, then why hadn't John ever heard of her? Brother Jim was smiling like he knew what John was thinking. Brother Jim stood up.

"Come with me," Brother Jim motioned for John to follow him back into the church. They walked into Jim's office. He pulled out a church directory and turned to the Sunday School pages. He began to point.

"Here is Tom, Amy, Leroy, Colt, David, Jason, and here, in the middle, is Veronica. Recognize her?"

John's mouth dropped.

"Brother Jim, that's . . ." John couldn't finish the sentence. Brother Jim nodded with a tight smile. Gears seemed to fall into place in John's mind. Things that made no sense, suddenly, were falling into place. The attempt to move Bruce into the lead investigator role on this case, now that move by Washington really made sense. The note that said "tell Veronica I know who she is" . . . then that meant . . . now John had a problem. He sat down in a chair in the preacher's office and began to think.

If he rushed back to New York, that would throw up too many red flags if he was being watched. With this level of involvement, he had to think he was. If John was to solve this case, he had to believe the men paid to protect Veronica would do their job. He didn't like it, but it was all he could do. He looked up at Brother Jim.

"John," began Brother Jim. "You have managed to stumble upon the one man who has put this all together, simply because I have information no one else has and what happened next in the story has kept me awake at night for over two decades. John, everyone in this town owes the Staples. Archibald saved this town. They won't look closely at what happened here. Some may know the truth, but they'll never tell. They don't know what happened, and if they did, I think they would be too scared something might happen to them to say anything. Honestly, I don't know for sure what happened, but I have a very good idea."

"You have more to tell me." It wasn't a question. John was sure there was more Jim knew, and even more Jim suspected.

Brother Jim nodded, "Let's go back outside, because, my friend, you ain't heard nothing yet."

Chapter 45

They walked back outside, but instead of stopping at the porch, Brother Jim pointed to a path across the road. John had a feeling; if they were going to be walking down a trail that was grown over with trees, shrubs, and grass, there was a very good reason. John stopped Brother Jim for a minute and ran back to the car. He pulled a small pouch out of his luggage that the forensics team had made up for him. It was the chemicals and a light pen used to test for human blood. He also grabbed two powerful flashlights. John had a bad feeling he was about to need it. He returned to Brother Jim and they resumed their walk. Jim resumed his story.

"John, I've told you all of this so that you can understand what I'm about to tell you. Beth and David George were good kids, but they were raised by a mother who only cared about herself. She was an alcoholic and who knows what other types of drugs she used. I'm honestly surprised she didn't contract some kind of STD with the amount of men she seemed to be with. Maybe that part isn't true; I can only go off of what the children told me."

Jim stopped. John waited; he was sure he was about to be hit with a bomb. The preacher looked so uncomfortable. When he started, he spoke very softly. There were tears in his eyes as he talked.

"John, you have to understand. Veronica saw the George's as her pets to parade around. She was making them out to be Americans who had overcome the odds of rural Kentucky. By this time, I knew not to cross Veronica, and so did most of the people in the town. The problem was Beth never saw that side of Veronica for all Veronica did for Beth and David." Tears began to flow freely down Jim's face.

"Beth." Jim's voice broke, he swallowed and continued. "Beth came to me." Jim looked away. When he turned to face John, John saw many, many years of regret in Jim's eyes. "John, she told me she was gay." John wasn't sure what he was expecting to hear, but it wasn't that. "I know what you're thinking, but hear me out," said Jim.

"The first thing I thought of was Beth's safety. It was the late 1980's, and kids had been killed before for their sexuality. But it wasn't the town I worried about. It was Veronica. Do you see, John? Beth was supposed to be her project. Beth was supposed to be the girl and David the boy, which overcame the odds. At that time in America, gays were not looked upon well. Do you understand John?"

John was trying to remember that time in his life. If Veronica was what Jim had described her to be, and John, so far, had no evidence that Jim was lying, Veronica would snap. Now other things were starting to fall into place. Why had John never heard the names of Beth and David George? Were they alive? John turned toward Jim and by the look on Jim's face he finally understood why they were walking in the woods.

"Jim?" John asked very calmly. "Where are David and Beth George?"

"John, no one knows."

John had stumbled onto one of the most politically radioactive cases since Nixon, and now realized that there may be a body count of seven.

Chapter 46

"Jim, did Veronica kill Beth and David?" John asked the question he wasn't for sure he could handle the answer to. If the answer was yes . . . John couldn't even begin to fathom what kind of fallout would follow. All John knew for sure was he wanted a drink.

"John," said Brother Jim. "I'll tell you the rest of what I know and then we can go from there. Beth insisted to me that she had to tell Veronica the truth. I tried to talk Beth out of it, but she wouldn't hear of it. She told me she didn't love Veronica, and she wasn't attracted to her. I tried to explain to her that didn't matter to Veronica, but Beth was sure Veronica would understand. I tried and I tried to stop her, but she refused. That was the last time I saw Beth or David."

"A few days later I went to their home. Mrs. George said that David and Beth had gone to live with their fathers, out of state. I went to the local sheriff and he went to talk to Mrs. George. Once again, she told him the same thing. Within the next two weeks, the parents of Tom, Amy, Leroy, and Colt all moved away; back to the states they came from, with promotions. Two weeks after that, Mr. Staples moved his family back to Virginia. There was never another mention of Veronica that I could find. In fact, I couldn't even find a birth certificate for her. Trust me I searched."

John was sick to his stomach. He couldn't believe what he was hearing. Two children disappeared, and it was, essentially, covered up. In fact, if someone hadn't murdered Tom, Amy, Leroy, and Colt, no one might have ever uncovered this mess. One last fact was tickling John's brain. He turned to Brother Jim, but Jim apparently was reading John's mind again.

"In the coming months," began Brother Jim, "any time anything was mentioned about the family of Mr.

Staples they would talk about being his daughter was Lisa Staples, who of course grew up and got married . . ."

"And became the First Lady of the United States of America, Lisa Nichols," finished John. "I need a drink."

Lisa Nichols (Veronica Staples)
1600 Pennsylvania Avenue

Chapter 47

Lisa slammed her fist against the desk. She had been going over the reports from the FBI. She was furious to learn that Bruce had not taken the case like she thought he would. This could complicate things. She straightened up and ran her hand through her hair. Who was she kidding? Lisa's life had been complicated ever since that selfish, redneck girl ruined her life.

"I rose up though, Beth, in spite of you. I was what you should have aspired to be." Lisa was giving herself another pep talk. Secret Service agents had learned over the years, unless the first lady actually called them by name, they were to ignore her when she got like this. Lisa was fired up today.

She sat down in her chair, and thought back to that terrible day that had nearly ruined her life before it even began. Lisa was in the mine. She thought of it as her kingdom. Beth had asked Lisa to meet her there. Lisa was supposed to come alone, but Lisa did as she pleased. She had brought Jason with her. Lisa and Jason needed to have a talk. Jason was going to be the star quarterback of the football team, and, for now, Jason would do nicely on her arm as eye candy. Lisa was going to convince Jason of this, however she had to.

When Lisa heard Beth coming, she sent Jason on into the dark tunnels and told him to wait until Beth left. It was a good thing she did. There was no telling what Beth might have done if Jason hadn't been there. Lisa remembered that was the last day anyone had ever called her Veronica. Lisa slid back into the memories.

128

Chapter 48

"Veronica," Beth called. Veronica waved Beth over to her rock throne. They had discovered the rock formation one day and had made this their clubhouse. They were always very careful, because 20 feet behind them was a hole in the ground. It was surrounded by a wall of wood, but the wood was rotten, and all of them kept waiting for the day it fell.

Beth walked up to Veronica, determined to tell her best friend what she had been keeping from her for months. Veronica would understand; she understood everything.

"Veronica, I have to tell you something very important," began Beth. She took a deep breath and told Veronica her most important, intimate secret. "Veronica, I'm gay. Now I'm not telling you this because I'm in love with you or anything like that. I'm telling you because you're my friend and I know you'll support me . . . Veronica? Veronica? What's wrong?"

Veronica was furious. It was obvious to her. Beth was going to tell everyone that the two of them were gay. No, it was even worse than that! People would assume Veronica was gay because she was friends with Beth. This would absolutely ruin her! How could she ever hope to be President of the United States if this ever came out? This redneck loser that Veronica had turned into a proper lady repaid her with this? No, Beth wasn't going to destroy everything Veronica had worked so hard for. No she wasn't! Veronica knew exactly how to fix things. Veronica began to scream.

"Help!" Veronica screamed. "Help me! She's raping me! She's trying to make me gay!" Beth had watched her friend turn a violet shade of red and then Veronica began this insane screaming. Didn't Veronica understand? Beth had told Veronica because she trusted her, and now Veronica was screaming nonsense about turning her gay? Did Veronica have any clue what Beth had shared with her; her most intimate secret? Beth tried to calm Veronica. Beth shushed Veronica and tried to put her hand over Veronica's mouth to quite her. As Beth did this, she saw an evil look come into Veronica's eyes. Veronica smashed her mouth against Beth's hand and started mumbling into it. If Beth didn't know better, it would seem like Veronica was making it look like Beth was trying to silence her; permanently. Then, to Beth's surprise, Veronica grabbed Beth's wrist. Veronica slammed Beth's hand up against her breast. If someone were to come into the room, it would look like Beth was sexually assaulting Veronica. What Beth didn't know, was Jason was just entering the room.

Chapter 49

Jason had heard Veronica's screams and came around the corner. He swore he heard Veronica scream she was being raped. He had to look twice at the scene he was witnessing. Beth had one hand over Veronica's face trying to keep Veronica quiet, and Beth's other hand was on Veronica's breast. Beth was trying to assault, or even rape, Veronica! Jason grabbed a rock and ran toward them. When he got behind Beth, he never said a word. He swung the rock, hitting Beth in the head. Beth fell like a lump of bricks. Veronica dropped to the ground, gasping.

"Jason!" Veronica was crying. "Jason, she was going to rape me!" Veronica ran up and hugged Jason. She smiled into his jacket. She dropped the smile and looked back up at Jason with her best terrified look. "Jason, we have to get rid of the body." Jason looked down in horror. Veronica took control of the situation.

"Jason, it's simple. Pick her up, and push her through the boards. She'll land on her back down there, and any injuries will look like she picked them up in the fall." Jason looked dumbfounded. She ran her hand up his arm. "Jason, you have to do this. Don't worry. I'll protect you. No one will find out." Jason nodded, and picked up Beth's lifeless body. He walked over to the boarded up mine shaft. He threw her off his shoulders so she would go through the boards back first.

As Beth crashed through the boards, Jason heard someone screaming, "NOOOO!!" and felt something hit him in the back. If Jason hadn't been so muscular from his years of playing football, he might have joined Beth going over the railing. As it was, his legs buckled and he dropped to the ground. Fists were pounding on Jason's back.

As this was going on, around the corner of the cavern came the group of Colt, Tom, Leroy and Amy. They were shocked to see Veronica on the ground weeping.

They were also surprised to see David George on Jason's back, beating on him with all his might. Veronica ran to the group.

"She tried to . . ." Veronica sobbed, and collected herself. "Beth tried to rape me and now David has attacked Jason!" Veronica stumbled away from the fight and the fell to the ground. The group gathered around her. While that was going on, Jason finally managed to throw the assaulter off of him.

Jason looked up and for the first time noticed it was David George. David began to circle Jason, neither one really paying any attention to their surroundings. Jason had about had it. First Beth had been assaulting his girl, and then this little trailer park punk attacked him. Jason lost it. He took both of his hands and shoved David right in the middle of his chest. It was then Jason realized they were standing right in front of the broken boards. Jason watched in horror as David went over the edge, just like David's sister did not two minutes earlier. Jason heard a sick thud from the bottom of the shaft.

Veronica whipped her head around when she heard the noise; everyone was looking at the hole and Jason. Veronica had to fight back an evil smile that flashed across her face. Jason fell to the ground and began to sob. In less than five minutes, Jason had killed two people.

The group was stunned. Veronica took control.

"Everyone, I need you to give us a few minutes. Please don't say a word to anyone about what happened here. We could get into a lot of trouble. Do you understand?" Everyone nodded. "We'll all get together in a little bit and figure out what to do." The group took off. Veronica came up to Jason and held him.

"Jason," she whispered. "Jason, you need to collect yourself." Jason looked up into Veronica's eyes, still sobbing. Veronica continued. "I'm sorry about Beth and

David, but they attacked us. Look, I thought the world of both of them, but they were going to grow up to be junkies or deadbeats just like their mother. You saved them from that. Don't forget who they were and what they were trying to do to me. I helped them, and they repaid me by trying to rape me." Jason nodded. Veronica kissed him softly on the lips. "Jason, I need you to go talk to everyone. Have them meet back here in two hours. I'll take care of everything, ok?" Jason nodded. Veronica kissed him again and Jason took off. Veronica knew what she had to do.

Chapter 50

Veronica stood outside of the George's home. She looked through the window of the trailer. There was David's and Beth's mother asleep or passed out, Veronica couldn't tell which, on the couch. Veronica tried the front door, and it opened. Veronica walked into the kitchen and started opening up cupboard doors. She found a bottle of vodka and walked outside. Veronica poured the vodka out of the bottle into some shrubbery behind the trailer. She started sobbing a little to make tears come to her eyes. She walked up to the door and started knocking. After thirty seconds or so, she started banging on the door.

Margery "Mag" George answered the door, looking like death warmed over. Veronica started to speak but began to bawl. Mag, not wanting to create a scene, quickly brought her inside.

"Mag," Veronica sobbed. "I'm so, so sorry. They're gone, Mag. They're gone."

Mag was fighting a serious hangover, but she was sober enough to get the drift. Mag sank to the couch. What would she do? Maybe she was misunderstanding. But if she wasn't, what would she do without the money she got from the government for those two little brats?

"Veronica, sweetie," Mag began. "I don't understand what is going on. Tell me exactly what happened."

Veronica went to sobbing just enough where she could talk. "I found this by the old mine shaft." She was holding up the empty vodka bottle. "The boards were broken. I think they drank the vodka and then . . . and then . . . they fell through!" Veronica sobbed hysterically. Mag was devastated. What would she do for money? The only steady income Mag had was the money she received for those two.

134

Mag began to panic. I'll have to get a full-time job, Mag thought. No, that wasn't possible; there was no way she could pass any drug test. Mag began to think her life was over, but then Veronica said something that made Mag think all her problems were solved.

"I'm gonna get in so much trouble for even showing them that shaft. If only there was something we could do where no one would miss them." And with that, Veronica baited the hook. Mag realized that Veronica and her family were loaded. "You know the only money I get was the money I got for the kids," Mag sobbed. Veronica looked at Mag through the tears in her eyes. Inside Veronica knew she had her.

"Mag, maybe Daddy could help you. I mean you've lost the only two children you have. You should be compensated in some way for that. What if he were to give you $10,000.00?" Veronica asked softly. Mag smiled. Veronica continued.

"Mag, you do realize if someone found the bodies of your children, you could face charges. You don't want to go to jail Mag." Mag shook her head no. Veronica pressed on. "Mag, you have to understand, if anyone were to find out what happened, you could go to jail for a very long time. People could say that you neglected your kids. They might make you take a drug test. Do you understand me, Mag?" Mag nodded. Veronica smiled and took Mag's hand into hers.

"You know? If anyone asks, you could just tell them that Beth and David went to live with their father . . . or fathers . . . however it worked out. No, I don't want to know. If I don't know, I can honestly tell people I don't know where they are. If anyone presses you on it, just tell them it's none of their business." Mag nodded.

"Do we have a deal?" Veronica put out her hand and Mag shook it. Veronica chuckled inside. She understood people and how their minds worked. They would sell anything for the right price. Apparently, the going rate to keep someone quiet about the death of two trailer park kids was $10,000.00.

Chapter 51

Veronica made her way to her father's office after leaving the trailer park. She was a little upset with herself. She probably could have gotten Mag to take less than $10,000.00 but it was done with little or no fuss. She thought Daddy would be pleased. She had taken a negative and turned it into a positive. She walked into the building and up to her father's office. The secretary saw her and nodded for her to go in. Veronica walked in, saw her father on the phone, shut the door and locked it. He father noticed her lock the door. He ended the call quickly, buzzed his secretary and told her to hold all of his calls. Her father offered her a seat. Veronica sat and then told her father everything. She didn't sugarcoat anything, and he didn't flinch with anything she said. When she finished, he sat quiet for a minute lost in thought. Then Veronica spoke again.

"Daddy, I think I messed up." Her father looked at her sharply. "I really believe Mag would have accepted $5,000.00, but I didn't want to take any chances." Her father smiled.

"Dear, there's a time when you have to pay a little more to get the desired outcome. In this case, I think that's perfectly fine. You were faced with a unique set of circumstances. I'm very proud of you. You didn't become emotional. You analyzed the situation and achieved the best possible outcome, exactly as I taught you. I assume you have a plan for taking care of everything else?"

"Of course," said Veronica. "I'll meet with the others, and let them know how bad it would be for all of us if they were to find those bodies. I have explained to Mag how it is possible she could be brought up on charges of neglect if anyone were to find the bodies. I suspect she'll be dead soon anyway. With that much money she's likely to overdose. I was thinking, in about two months, if it wouldn't cause you too much trouble, we could have all the parents of the others sent back to their original homes with a promotion. Then a month later, we could move back to Virginia. My running for president is out of the question, but I could become the first lady. Do you know anyone who could change my name?"

He father beamed at her. "Dear, well thought out. Very well done! I have a few friends in the DOJ that can help with the name change. I am assuming you are doing it to make sure no one can ever link you back to this town?"

"Yes daddy. I was thinking we could falsify some school records showing that I was taught with a private tutor until I start school in Virginia. That way if anyone ever comes looking for me, I don't exist."

Archibald nodded. "It will take a little doing to get the birth records straightened out, but that shouldn't be a problem. Are you sure they're both dead?"

Veronica frowned. "Well, I didn't see them, but I'm almost sure that Beth was dead when Jason struck her from behind. There was an awful sound of bones breaking when the boy went over the side. I can't see how he could have survived that fall, but it was too dark down the hole to see for sure. Do you want me to go back and look?"

Archibald waved off the suggestion. "No, Veronica, if they survived the fall, I'm sure they both are dead from their injuries by now."

"Daddy, call me Lisa." Her father was confused for just a second and then realized what she had done. He roared with laughter.

"That's my girl! Cutting your losses and moving on! Well, we can't call you Lisa until we get you to Virginia, but if Lisa is the name you want, then I will get it started. I'll also have a talk with the local police and sheriff to make sure that if anyone comes around asking or suggesting anything, it is properly ignored."

Veronica stood up to leave. Archibald stood as well and reached across the desk. He took hold of his daughter's wrist.

"Veronica, two people are dead today. Are you sure you're ok?"

Veronica looked her father in the eyes; her stare was of blue steel. "Daddy, I tried to make their lives better and all they did was ruin mine. They're lucky that dying was all that happened to them. No one ever crosses me and gets away with it." Her father let go of her wrist and gave her a big beaming smile. Veronica crossed the office and unlocked the doors. Her father picked up the phone and made a call. As she shut the door she heard her father talking to Fred. She didn't know his last name, or his exact title. He was simply known as the Cleaner. She hated that someone else had to clean up her mess, or that she had a mess at all. As she walked out of the building, all she could think was sometimes you have to break a few eggs to make an omelet.

Chapter 52

Veronica met with Tom, Colt, Leroy, Amy, and Jason. She knew this was the last thing she had to take care of. They met back in the cave. The group stayed away from the shaft that David and Beth had fallen through to their death. They all seemed a little spooked by the broken boards that were in front of the hole. Veronica thought about peering down to see if she could see the bodies, but decided that would just be too morbid. Honestly, she thought, how could anyone survive that fall?

"Everyone," Veronica started. "I need you to listen to me. What happened here today was terrible. What I'm going to say may sound harsh, but it's only because it's the truth, and many times the truth is harsh. I am sorry those two died earlier, but we can't have our lives ruined over an accident. Now we could go to the police, but there is the chance they would arrest Jason. That would ruin any chance he has of being the starting quarterback next year. Jason has a chance to go to college on a football scholarship." Veronica knew she had to make everyone understand that this was for everyone, not just Jason.

"Amy, you want to be a teacher. Tom, you want to be a doctor. Colt, you want to be an accountant, and Leroy." Veronica smiled as she looked at Leroy. "Leroy, do you think an amusement park for kids would hire someone that was involved with a questionable death?" Veronica looked around at all of them. "Do any of you think the profession you want to be in would?" She let the question hang in the air. "Look, as long as we don't talk, no one will ever know. I know David's and Beth's mother won't talk. She won't go to the police because she's afraid she'll be arrested for neglect." Veronica looked around at the group; she could see the agreement growing on their faces. She had to bring it home. She was proud of herself for leading the group exactly where she needed them to be.

She was especially happy with herself because she knew her father would be so proud.

"I hate to even mention this, but Beth was trying to rape me . . . " Veronica started a fake sob to gain a little sympathy. She collected herself and continued. "Apparently she made her brother follow her to help if needed. There is no telling what those two deviants would have done to me if Jason hadn't saved me. They would have ravaged me, and then . . ." She gave a shudder. "And then for all I know they may have thrown me through that shaft."

Veronica looked over the group. If she couldn't become the first lady, then she had no doubt she could be a great trial lawyer. No one could out argue her.

"Does anyone disagree with anything I've said here?" She looked around and they all shook their heads. They didn't like it, but she had convinced them. "Ok, here's what's going to happen. To protect everyone, all of your parents are going to be transferred back to the original state you came from." Jason looked crestfallen. Veronica put her hand on his knee. He raised his head and looked into her eyes. Veronica talked very softly. "Jason, please understand this kills me. We have to do it though; it's to protect your future. It's to protect all of us. We have to forget about each other. Once we each move away, do not contact me ever again." The group looked shocked. "I know this seems harsh, but I plan to be a public figure one day, and I don't want to go through the constant questions of what happened to me today. It would be too hard. I don't think I could take the constant questions. Nothing happened to me today, but the press will try to sensationalize it. I don't want to be one of those people who are connected to something when I was never actually raped. Do you understand?"

Everyone nodded. Veronica knew they were still in shock and this was the best time to get everyone to agree. Veronica stood up and hugged each of them. The group began to break up and leave. Jason lingered until everyone left. He tried to approach Veronica, but she simply shook her head no, and pointed toward the exit. Jason nodded and walked away.

For the most part, that was the last time Veronica ever saw them alive again. She stayed away from the group over the next few weeks as the transfer orders for the group's parents took place. Veronica's father announced that he was moving his family back to Virginia a few days after the last parent was transferred. The day Veronica got in the car to leave Kentucky was the last day anyone ever called her by that name. On that day, Lisa was born.

Chapter 53

Lisa looked up at the clock. An hour had passed. She hadn't thought about that day for over twenty-five years. She could never forgive Beth and David for costing her a shot at the presidency. There was no way she could ever run with what had happened. Lisa felt secure the identity that was built for her was fool proof, but she didn't want to chance it. She was afraid nothing would hold up to the scrutiny of the media if she were to have run for the nation's highest office. She knew her only chance was to be the first lady. She had hopes of being Secretary of State someday, but anything more than that was now impossible. She was so angry at the George siblings for destroying her dreams. She sent an instant message for Agent McDonald to come to her office immediately.

A few minutes later there was a knock on the door and Agent McDonald entered. Lisa knew she couldn't personally get too involved with the FBI or someone would start to wonder why she was involved. She needed Luke to take care of this for her. She had to stress that to Agent McDonald. When Luke entered, Lisa walked to the door and locked it. Agent McDonald stood there frozen like a statue. Lisa walked up beside him and ran her hand down his arm.

"Luke," Lisa purred. "I need you to get Agent Fowler off of this case. If I understand right, Bruce Cosby turned it down. Maybe you need to talk to Senator Cosby. I can't believe a father wouldn't want to see his son succeed."

Luke swallowed nervously, "Mrs . . . " Lisa cut him off.

"Luke, call me Lisa, or when we're alone, Silk." Lisa smiled at Luke seductively.

"Lisa . . . I talked to Agent Cosby, and if I understand him right, he and his father don't get along."

Lisa moved from Luke's shoulder to stand right in front of him. Lisa straightened Luke's tie and then raised her eyebrows twice, very quickly. She mocked at undoing Luke's tie. Luke thought he might pass out. If anyone were to walk in . . .

"Let me guess," Lisa inquired. "Bruce wants Daddy to approve, right?" Luke nodded. "Then talk to Senator Cosby, and if that doesn't work . . . maybe do something that would help Bruce impress Daddy. I'll make sure nothing happens to you if you take care of this. Do we understand each other, Luke?"

Luke nodded. He knew exactly what he could do. He would get Senator Cosby to help him with Bruce. If Senator Cosby wouldn't assist Luke with Bruce, then Luke would "kidnap" the senator. Not for real. He would take the senator without Jeremiah knowing it was Luke. Luke could use a mask or something to disguise his identity from the senator. Luke would feed Bruce the information of where the senator was so Bruce could "rescue" him. Luke looked Lisa up and down. Lisa winked at him and waved him away. As Luke left, he wondered how far "Silk" was willing to go.

John Fowler
Kentucky

Chapter 54

John was sitting beside the cave entrance. He was sick to his stomach. If all of this was true . . . he looked up at Brother Jim.

"Jim, let me run through this from start to finish to make sure I completely understand." Jim nodded. "Jason Sparks, Beth George, and David George were born and raised here in this town. Archibald Industries came here, and Lisa Staples moved here when her father, The Archibald Staples, moved to the community. Archibald brings several people from other plants whose children include Tom, Amy, Leroy, and Colt; the four people killed at Jason Sparks' funeral. Veronica Staples starts to try and "save" Beth George, in her eyes, by making Beth the girl who beat the odds of a single, possibly drunk and drug addled parent from rural Kentucky." Jim nodded, John continued. "The last time anyone ever saw Beth was when she came to you to tell you she was gay. She told you she was going to meet Veronica. There has never been any follow up by the police, when you talked to them, except that they told you Mrs. George stated her two children went to live with their fathers. Two weeks after you last saw Beth, the parents of the four murdered mourners moved back to their home states. Then Archibald leaves Kentucky and the next thing you know, Veronica Staples has disappeared from all public record and Lisa has taken her place." John stopped, exhausted.

"John, you got it, sadly, that is it exactly," said Brother Jim. John shook his head. He had stepped in it, and it stank high to heaven. They both stared at the cave entrance. Brother Jim looked at the flashlights John had been carrying. John sighed and nodded his head. He handed Brother Jim a flashlight and they started inside. Brother Jim stopped at each branch within the cavern and looked for markings. John smiled; it was like something out of a Mark Twain novel. They followed the markings and entered a large room. Inside the large room, John looked around with his flashlight. He saw torches in the wall and a stone that resembled a throne. He continued to look and noticed an old rotted wooden barrier; one side was broken. John looked over the side with his flashlight. He called Brother Jim over and they both shined their flashlights down the hole. John lowered his head. He was pretty sure he could see a skull sticking up out of what looked to be a shallow pool. Brother Jim was on one knee.

"John, is that . . ." Brother Jim tried to ask. John nodded.

"I only saw one. Jim, did you see another?" John asked. Jim shook his head no. John swung his flashlight around. He was trying to see if there was a trail to the broken boards. He got up and walked toward the back of the cave, looking for anything. He pulled out his spray, and moistened the broken boards. He sprayed around the ground and worked his way back out until he ran out of the chemicals. He put on the special glasses and did find some flecks of blood where the boards were broken, but not the amount he expected. He kept using his light as he walked away from the hole, and found a small pool about thirty feet away from the mine shaft. John nodded, and turned to Brother Jim.

"Jim, I need you to do something that may be very hard. I need you to not tell a soul about this." Jim looked surprised. "If this goes the way you and I are thinking, the last thing we need to do is involve the local police. I'm

146

going back to New York. I'll get a team together and they'll be down here by the end of next week. Whatever, excuse me, whoever, is down there has obviously been there for years, so a week isn't going to hurt."

Jim looked at the hole and back to John. "John, do you think she's involved?" John shook his head, looked at the hole and then back to Jim.

"Jim, I have no idea, but if she is, then you understand the need for secrecy, right?" Jim nodded. "Let's get out of here." The two of them left the cave and headed back to the church. They didn't say anything during the walk. When they reached the church, John shook Brother Jim's hand.

"Jim, I know you think this is on you, but that isn't the case," said John. "Veronica, or Lisa, or whoever she is. That's the person behind all of this." John put his hand on Jim's shoulder. "You're a good man, Jim. Never forget that." Jim nodded. John got in the car and headed down the road toward the interstate. As the town disappeared in his rearview mirror, all John could think about was how at least six deaths were possibly responsible by something the current first lady had done.

"John, when you find a case to come back with, you find a case to come back with," John said to no one in particular.

Chapter 55

As John headed down the road, he began to wonder where he was going. His flight wasn't leaving until tomorrow night. He could simply go to a hotel near the airport and relax for a few days. The other option was for him to go see his parents. He looked over at the seat beside him halfway expecting to see Sam. She wasn't there. John wasn't sure if he was glad, or not, that she wasn't. John sighed, entered his parents address into the GPS, and turned on the satellite radio. John headed down the road, ready for the two and a half hour drive.

Two hours later, as he got off the interstate and turned away from town, nervousness began to gnaw at him. He assumed his parents would gladly see him. What if they wanted nothing to do with him? John tried to shake that thought from his mind.

He passed the high school on the outskirts of town and turned onto the road that would lead to his parents' house. As he looked over the countryside, he turned nostalgic of the people that lived there when he was growing up. He turned off the main road a couple of minutes later and drove past the church he grew up in. John navigated the car through the twisty, windy road. He topped a hill and turned his car onto the last turn before he came to his parents' house. He drove down the road and started down the hill. He made the turn at the base of the hill to his parents' farm. As he pulled up into the drive, memories overwhelmed John.

John parked the car, turned off the engine, and got out of the car. The side door of the house opened, and there was his father. His father raised his eyebrows in surprise and headed down the walk toward him. His dad stuck out his hand toward him. "Bubba." His father said. It was a joke between them from John's teenage years. Henry, John's father, called John "Bubba," and John called his father "George." They had gotten those names from a cartoon the two had been watching one Saturday morning when John was growing up waiting for a Cats game to start. "George," John responded. John caught his father in a bear hug, and his father was taken off guard for a second. His father hugged him back, and patted John's back. John was near tears.

"George . . . Dad . . . I'm sorry," John tried to say without losing his composure.

"It's alright, son. It's alright. Welcome home."

Chapter 56

John and his father walked inside. He heard rustling farther on in the house.

"Henry," John's mother called. "Is someone there?"

"It's John," Henry simply replied. John's mother burst around the corner of the kitchen and came into view. Tears were in her eyes. John tried to speak, but couldn't. He simply walked across the room and hugged his mother.

"I'm sorry, Mom, for what I said to you at the funeral," John said.

John's mother pulled away from him and looked at John. "As well you should, young man!" His mother admonished. She smiled at John and hugged him again. "John, you went through something Henry and I have never experienced and couldn't imagine living through. What happened that day is forgiven, and forgotten."

John smiled at his mother. His parents invited him into the living room. John walked into the living room and looked around. It was like he never left. He sat on the couch and answered all of their questions of what had been going on in his life. They were somewhat disappointed he had left the FBI, but very excited about him working on the current case. They talked for a couple of hours and it was starting to get late. John stood up to leave.

"And just where do you think you're going, young man?" His mother asked.

"I figured I had better get into town and get me a room," John answered.

"John Fowler!" His mother exclaimed. "You sit down right this second. You'll stay here tonight and that will be the end of it!" John looked over at this father. His father was sitting in the recliner, leaning in toward the couch listening to and joining into the conversation when he had something to add. When John looked over at him, his father straightened and shook his head.

"You heard your mother. I'm not getting dragged into that fight. No matter how it would end, I would lose," Henry said. John smiled. Over three years and things hadn't changed at all.

"Besides," said his mother. "You have to tell me how you and Jessica are doing and when you plan on getting on with your life and marrying that girl." John's mouth dropped. Henry barked a laugh. John's mother walked into the kitchen. "I've got some homemade pimento cheese, John, would you like a sandwich?" John, with his mouth still opened, turned toward his father. Henry smiled. He leaned in toward John and spoke where only John could hear him.

"Bubba, you better answer her . . . and tell her if you want the pimento cheese as well." Henry leaned back, smiling broadly.

"Yes, Mom, I'd like a sandwich," John answered. John shook his head, chuckling to himself. As much as things had changed since Sam's death, the more they had stayed the same.

Chapter 57

John walked into the kitchen as his mom was making him a sandwich.

"Mom," said John. "Let me do that. I'm almost forty years old."

His mother ignored him and continued making the sandwich. "John, I'm your mother. If I want to make my baby boy a sandwich, then I will. If I don't want to, I'll tell you to make it yourself! Now shut up and eat!" She placed the sandwich on a plate and handed it to him. John took it to the table and began to eat. His mom sat down at the table and watched him. John put down the sandwich.

"How do you know about Jessica, Mom, and what exactly do you mean when am I going to marry her?" He asked.

"After the funeral that day," his mother began. "Jessica came up to me and said she was a friend of both you and Sam. She said you didn't really know about her and Sam's relationship. She also said that you were suffering from alcoholism due to you being undercover. John, she told me everything." His mother looked away for a minute. When she looked back she had tears in her eyes. "John, she has been the only contact I've had with you for three years. I haven't seen you since you were drunk at your own wife's funeral!" John felt about three inches tall. He started to speak, but his mother stopped him.

"John, we didn't know what was going on. She took us to dinner after you left and explained your undercover work and how you had to get into the mob. She said one of downfalls of going undercover is some cops or FBI agents succumb to drugs and alcohol. John, I understand why you did it, and I understand why you were so hurt. Jessica told me how she was the one to interview you over the death of your wife. She said she couldn't reveal a lot of what happened, but the gist of what she said was you blamed yourself for Sam's death. John, it's not your fault."

"I know that now, Mom," said John quietly.

"Good," said his Mother patting him on the shoulder. "Have you forgiven Jessica?" John nodded. "Good! Now what is going on with you two?" John about choked.

"Mom," John began but didn't know what to say. His mom smiled.

"John," began his mother. "This woman has talked to me about you for three years. Do you know she was talking to me one night and she was upset about dating Chit?"

"You mean Chet?" asked John.

"Oh yes, that's what I meant." John laughed; his mother shushed him and continued. "She told me she was worried that she was dating him to find out about you." John groaned.

"Mom," John began. "I do not want to discuss my love life, or lack thereof, with you. I don't know what to do about Jessica. I loved my wife, and I made her miserable because of my being undercover." John's father had been listening in the doorway.

"Do you think our marriage has been unicorns and dandelions?" His father asked. John was shocked. "For being a great detective, you're an idiot sometimes. People make each other mad and upset. It's part of life. What makes marriages work is to work through the problems. What you're hung up on, if you want my opinion, and I'm gonna give it to you whether you want it or not, because you need to hear this; you're problem, John, is you two were having trouble and then she died." Henry paused. John looked down at the floor, ashamed. He had spent three years beating himself up over what happened and an afternoon with his parents gave him more clarity than anything had since Sam's death. Henry continued.

"You had a drinking problem, Son. Were you going to do something about it?" Henry asked.

John took a deep breath fighting back tears. "I was going to her that night to tell her I was joining AA and was leaving the FBI. I was literally a block away from the apartment to tell her all of this when I saw it blow up."

Tears welled up in John's eyes. His mother got up and hugged him from the left side while his father put his hand on John's right shoulder. They were quiet for a few moments. His mom let him go, and sat back down. His dad pulled up the chair beside him and sat down. His mom spoke.

"John, what happened was terrible, but from what I know of Sam, she wouldn't want you to be alone if being with someone else would make you happy. Does she? John, does Jessica make you happy?"

"Mom," John began. "I don't know. I don't know if I trust myself enough to put Jessica through the mess I would be if we began dating."

"You're not even dating?!" His mother exclaimed. "John, have you been on a date since Sam died?" John shook his head no. "JOHN EDWARD FOWLER!" Henry tried to calm his wife but she waved him off. After being married for over forty years, Henry knew when to let her go. "What would Sam say? Would she want you wallowing around in depression? Would she want you to just exist? Well?" Edna was fired up. John knew he was defeated. He smiled at his mother. "John, you take that girl out on a proper date!"

"Yes, Mom," John said smiling. His mother nodded. "Mom, I've had a long day. Do you mind if I hit the bed?" Edna smiled and got up to check his bedroom to make sure it met her satisfaction. Henry got up and was chuckling. John sat there for a minute.

"Home sweet home," John said out loud to no one.

Chapter 58

John got up the next morning, showered, dressed, and went outside to look over the farm. His dad hadn't worked the farm since before Sam had died. Henry had become disabled due to a disease he had contracted when John was eight. Henry walked out and was talking to John about the changes on the farm. John looked over where the grain bins used to be. His father sold them a few years ago. The barn was starting to fall apart. Henry told him the barn hadn't contained any hogs in years.

"Dad," John asked, "Do you think I can lead a normal life with Jessica, given how my life with Sam ended?"

"John," said his father. "You'll never know until you try. You know you're not as damaged, or messed up as you think you are." John looked at his father. "You have a problem, and you know about it. You're better off than many people. So many people have problems and can't admit it. So you struggle with it every day." Henry shrugged his shoulders for effect. He turned toward John. "Many people struggle with things every day. You have to live John; this life is too short."

John spoke, "Dad I'm sorry for not coming home sooner." His father looked at him, and drank from his coffee mug. He lowered the mug and looked out over the farm.

"Bubba, life is also way too short to apologize for a bunch of stupid mistakes made at bad places in our lives," said Henry. "We're family John, and family tends to screw up with family. Now don't you need to be getting to the airport?" John nodded. He hugged his dad and started back toward the house. "John," Henry called after him. John turned and Henry walked up to him. "What about Sam's death? Has it ever been solved?" John looked down at the ground. John kicked the ground and then looked back at his dad.

"Dad, there is a file on her, and I have been offered full use of the FBI if I decide to pursue the case. The problem is, Dad, I'm too close to it." Henry nodded.

"John, sometimes there are no answers. You know yourself better than anyone else. If you don't think you can do it without it causing yourself problems, specifically if it would lead you back to drinking, then you don't need to do it." John nodded. Henry put his hands on John's shoulders. "Son, she would understand. I mean that about everything." John nodded. "Son, ask the girl out!" John roared with laughter. Henry had a wide smile across his face and his eyes were dancing.

John walked back up to the house, and hugged his mom and his dad. He got in the car and headed back to the airport. It was a long drive. He needed it. He needed to decide what he was going to say to Jessica when he got home. He pulled out his cell phone and called her.

"Jessica, it's John," said John.

"Well thanks for that," she replied. "I mean this thing called caller ID did say you were John, but it could have been a stalker that wanted to ravage my body . . . of course you could be that stalker."

John swallowed. He knew she was just carrying on in their usual banter, but he didn't have it in him to do that right now. John summoned up all his nerve.

"Jessica," he paused. "Jessica I need to talk to you. May I come by your place tonight when I get back into town?"

There was silence on the other end. John felt like his heart was about to thump out of his chest. On the other end of the phone call, Jessica was grinning like a Cheshire cat. She knew John was trying to be sincere. She knew that she shouldn't torment him, but she wanted to dish out a little of what John had dished out over the years.

"Are you planning on ravaging my body?" She asked coyly. John nearly wrecked the car. He laughed. He couldn't help himself. He knew she was trying to give him grief. John only knew of one way to combat this. Fight fire with fire.

"Well, I didn't have it on the agenda, but if that's what it takes to seal the deal, then I'll see what I can do," he replied. Jessica knew she shouldn't go any farther, but sometimes, you do things you shouldn't.

"Great, I'm sure it will be like most men who talk a big game. I'll be thoroughly disappointed," she said. There was silence. Jessica silently chided herself. She knew she had gone too far. What she heard next caught her completely off guard.

John spoke barely above a whisper. "Jessica, if you should ever get the privilege of there being a you and me, I will personally guar, an, tee," he stressed each syllable. "The last thing in this world you will be is disappointed. I'll see you tonight." John hung up. Jessica sat on the phone staring into space. She began to fan herself with the hand not holding the phone. "Oh my," she said. She let her mind begin imagining. "Oh. My."

Chapter 59

Jessica was standing in the FBI building in New York, looking at her phone. John's call had ended five minutes ago. She had been leaning against a desk talking to John. She stood up and walked out the door to the elevator. She rode the elevator upstairs. She got out of the elevator and paused. What she was about to do might very well end her FBI career, but she had to though. She had to follow the proper protocols and tell what was going on. Whatever happened; she would deal with the consequences. She summoned all her courage and walked down the hall and into Trip's office.

"Trip, I may be about to enter into a relationship with another FBI officer. Well, he's not technically a FBI officer now, but after this case is over, I think he will be." Jessica was mad at herself. She was rambling. No one made her ramble, especially not that John Fowler. She smiled inside. Yes he did. She got herself together and continued. "I have no idea what all it is going to entail, but I need to report this." Jessica stood there waiting for Trip's response. Trip continued to work on paperwork, oblivious to Jessica's presence. Trip looked up and seemed startled to see her.

"Jessica," Trip said. "I'm so glad you're here. I've been meaning to talk to you about something. I was reading some things out of Washington the other day. Do you know that if no one reports a relationship between two people I cannot get in trouble if they were to continue to work together? So, say someone was to date someone. Let's say you and John, if he were a FBI agent, were to date. Let's just say, for fun, you two date and I never, ever, EVER was told about it. Do you know there would be nothing I could really do? I mean, if I found out on the day of the wedding, I guess I could come to the ceremony. At that point, I really don't see how I could tear apart their team. In other words, Agent, if you were to enter into a relationship with someone, I don't want to hear about it, especially since I never heard you might be in a relationship. Are we clear?" Jessica nodded. She started to leave.

"Jessica," Trip said quietly. She turned around to see a smile on his face. "Good luck." Jessica smiled and left Trip's office. Trip smiled thinking it was good that things were looking up around the office. A shadow darkened his door and there was a knock. Bruce stood there. Trip felt his smile leave.

"Bruce."

"Trip, everything alright?" Bruce asked.

"Everything is fine, Bruce," Trip replied.

Bruce smiled. "That's good to hear. Thought I heard shouting. Guess I was wrong. Have a good day, Trip." Bruce waved and headed down the hall without waiting to see Trip's reaction. Bruce walked down the hall. So John had a new girl. Bruce had hoped that John would drink himself into a stupor and walk out into traffic after Sam had died.

"You can't win them all," Bruce thought to himself. He patted his breast pocket as if feeling for something. He found what he was looking for and smiled. "I'm going to have to keep an eye on this situation."

Chapter 60

John stood outside of Jessica's apartment building. If it wasn't as cold as it was outside, he would have been sweating. John took a deep breath and walked inside. He went to the elevator and took it to her floor. As he got to her door, he heard music from inside. He recognized the song as something that Sam had listened to. John knocked on the door and there was no answer. He waited a minute and tried the knob. As he opened the door, what he saw surprised him.

On the screen was that blond singer that John could never remember, dancing with some snake. The bass of the song was shaking John. What stunned him was Jessica dancing to the music. She was amazing. John wasn't normally a fan of dance, but Jessica was very good. John felt his heart pounding in his chest. Jessica saw him during one of her moves. She smiled and kept dancing. John sat down in a chair that was near the door, mesmerized by how good she was.

When the song ended, Jessica grabbed a towel and was drying herself off. She was sweating, profusely. John thought he was going to begin sweating as well. She wasn't dressed provocatively; she was wearing a pair of spandex shorts and a tank top. Her hair was put up in a bun on her head.

"I didn't know that about you," said John. "I didn't know you could dance; that's real dancing!"

"I have been dancing since I was five, John," Jessica replied. "I love it. It keeps me in shape. I have learned hip-hop, ballet, jazz, and tap," Jessica smiled.

"Jess," John said. "That was absolutely amazing. I mean all I know is that little four step thing I learned at the school dance in middle school." Jessica laughed.

"I'm sorry, John. I lost track of time," she said. "Would it be ok if I took a shower before we talked?"

161

"Sure, Jess, take your time," John responded.

"I can trust you not to try and barge in, right?" Jessica asked. John looked hurt and did a "who me?" motion. Jessica wagged a finger at him warningly.

"Mind if I watch TV?" John called after her.

"Knock yourself out!" She called back. John flipped on the TV and found a college basketball game. John started to engross himself into the game, trying to forget how nervous he was to talk to Jessica.

Chapter 61

"John," Jessica called from her bedroom. "Are we planning on going out?"

"Huh?" said John, engrossed in the game. Jessica walked out of her bedroom, picked up the remote and turned off the TV. John was snapped back to reality and why he was here. He turned toward Jessica. She was dressed in a tee shirt and a pair of sweatpants. It was probably the most dressed down John had ever seen her. He thought she looked as beautiful as ever. "Oh crap," he realized, "I'm staring." Jessica wasn't going to let this one go easily.

"John," she said as sweetly as she could. She sat down beside him and took his hands. "John. Sweetie, we need to set some ground rules. I have no problem if you drop your jaw when I'm dressed up and looking my best, but it really hurts your credibility when you drool over me in a tee shirt and some sweats." Jessica was really enjoying this. John looked into Jessica's eyes.

"I'm sorry, Jessica. You're just beautiful no matter what you're wearing." Jessica dropped his hands. Jessica's mind started racing.

"Jessica," she thought to herself. "This guy means what he says." She was looking directly into John's eyes. Her heart was about to pound through her chest. "Calm down, calm down," she thought.

"John," said Jessica. "I don't know what to say. I've had guys tell me that before, but they were only after one thing. You seem to be honest and mean it. I'm flattered. Thank you."

"Jessica, you realize if you and I are to try this thing, it's going to be harder than most relationships you've ever been in. I mean, we could work together."

"Oh really?" Jessica said slyly.

John ignored the comment and continued. "You have to think of the pressure it will cause me. I mean, can I handle an adult relationship? I didn't fix the problems at the end of my last relationship." Jessica raised her eyebrows as John rambled. John didn't seem to notice and rambled on. "I mean we have to seriously ask, will I escape this relationship with alcohol if things start to go bad?" Jessica leaned across the couch and kissed him. John's mind exploded. It had been a long time . . . well, since Sam . . . that he had been kissed like that. In fact, he was pretty sure Sam had never kissed him like that.

Chapter 62

Jessica tenderly pulled away from John. Jessica had to admit that was one of the best kisses she had ever had in her life. Heck, it may be THE best kiss she ever had in her life. John couldn't believe what just happened. He had to remind himself to breathe.

"Thank you," he muttered. Jessica burst into laughter. John couldn't help himself and joined in. They laughed for several minutes; the tension in the room easing.

"I don't ever think anyone has ever thanked me for kissing them before," Jessica stated between laughs.

"I don't think anyone ever kissed me well enough to thank before," said John.

"Even Sam?" Jessica asked. She kicked herself after asking that. It was wrong of her on several levels for asking that.

John reached out and took Jessica's hand. "I honestly don't think so," John said quietly. "Sam and I had a different relationship. Don't get me wrong, Jessica. What Sam and I had was special and once in a lifetime, but I don't think she ever kissed me like that."

Jessica put her other hand over John's. "I kissed you to see if it was even worth us having this conversation," said Jessica.

John smiled wirily. "And your findings?" John asked. Jessica smiled broadly.

"Yeah," Jessica replied. John started laughing again, and Jessica joined in. When she could talk, she squeezed both of his hands in hers. "John, let's take this slow." John pulled his hands out of hers and stood up. Jessica was suddenly afraid she had upset him. John smiled and began to walk behind her couch.

"I need to say a few things, ok?" Jessica nodded. "I know about you talking to my mom." Jessica froze. "Oh crap" she thought, "I'm about to get it." Jessica prepared herself to receive a severe butt chewing by John.

Chapter 63

John smiled to himself. He knew he could lay into Jessica right now and she would take it, but it was time to do what needed to be done.

"Thank you," John said. "Thank you for letting my mom know when I couldn't. Thank you for being brave enough to take me into that box and proving beyond a shadow of a doubt that I didn't kill Sam. Thank you for believing in me enough to pull me back into the FBI and to a real life." John was smiling and his eyes were dancing.

"Jessica, I feel like me again. Yeah, I'm sad some days, and I swear I will call you a liar if you ever repeat what I'm about to tell you. The other day I saw Sam in my car." Jessica tried to fight a grin. John kept looking at her and she slowly put her finger up to her head and made the crazy sign. She was smiling at him. "I'm not crazy, or mad, or loony. I feel like me; you don't know how that feels after what I've been through." Jessica stood up and took his hands into hers.

"John," she began. "I had never seen two people love each other like you and Sam. If you didn't know, she understood the drinking. She wasn't mad, she didn't hate you, and she was willing to do anything to help you beat it. She was thinking about the two of you moving back to Kentucky. She thought being home would help you beat it. John, she loved you with all her heart. When I slapped you a few days ago, part of it was because I was mad at you for dishonoring her memory for the way you lived your life. I'll tell you the truth John, if the roles had been reversed, your death probably would have caused the same reaction in her."

John brushed the hair away from her face that had fallen there. He hated himself for what he was about to say.

"Jessica," he said very quietly. "I can't do this yet. I need to get through this case. I want there to be an us, but we need to get through this case. Do you understand?"

"I understand, John, but I don't have to like it," Jessica said holding his hands and drawing near. Her lips were inches from his. "We'll do whatever you need to do to get through this, at whatever speed you need to. For instance if you told me right now you needed to kiss me to get through the night, then I would understand."

John's heart was about to burst through his chest it was beating so hard. Jessica had a playful grin flickering across her face. John pushed her away. Jessica laughed loudly.

"You're enjoying this aren't you?" John asked. Jessica nodded. John walked to the door with Jessica right behind him. He opened it and turned around, once again his lips inches from hers.

"I promise you, Jess, it will be worth the wait," he said very quietly. He turned and left. Jessica closed the door and leaned back against it. Oh. Boy. This was gonna be interesting.

Agent Luke McDonald
Washington, DC

Chapter 64

Senator Cosby stood on the steps of the Lincoln Memorial. He was intrigued by the phone call he had received earlier by Secret Service Agent McDonald. Luke had wanted to meet with Jeremiah, but in a discreet location. Senator Cosby looked around and scoffed. He was chuckling over the ridiculous cloak and dagger operation that Agent McDonald appeared to be running. As McDonald appeared, Cosby vented some of his frustration.

"What do you think this is, Son?" The senator had lost all of his patience. "Is this some bad retelling of a crazy movie plot?"

Luke looked around to make sure no one heard Cosby. This caused Cosby to scoff at the whole thing even more.

"Senator," said Luke trying to calm Cosby down. "Certain people I work for need your help on a very delicate matter."

"You mean the president wants a favor," exclaimed Cosby.

"Sir!" said McDonald. "Please, keep your voice down, and no, it's not the president."

Cosby was bothered by that revelation. If Luke wasn't here for the president, Cosby was almost positive who he was there for.

"Luke, you can tell her that anyone related to Archibald Staples will get no help from me!" Senator Cosby exclaimed.

"Wait, sir, hear me out." Luke was nervous, he was about to lose Cosby without even telling him what was going on.

"All that we are asking of you, sir, is to suggest to the FBI that your son should take over a certain quadruple homicide case currently being investigated by John Fowler. We would also like it if you were to encourage your son to take the case if he is offered it."

Jeremiah laughed, turned, and walked away. As Senator Cosby disappeared into the night, Luke pulled out his cell phone and dialed a phone number given to him by Lisa.

"Sir, this is Luke McDonald. I work as a Secret Service Agent for Lisa. Yes, sir, she told me to call you if I needed any help." Luke continued to discuss plans with the man on the other end of the phone call.

Chapter 65

Trip, Jessica and Chet were already in the office when John came in. John asked them all to have a seat. As he began to lay out what had happened in Kentucky, the looks of disbelief and shock covered their faces. Trip was absolutely stunned. When John had finished, no one said a word for a minute. Then Trip spoke.

"John," Trip stopped, shook his head in disbelief again, and continued. "If what you're saying is true . . . if . . . John you can't just say those things. We need concrete proof! We have to have iron clad proof to go after her."

"I think I have all the proof you need sir, and furthermore, if John Fowler says something happened, well, then I believe him." Trip turned. John had a big grin on his face. Jeremiah Cosby had just walked through the door, but instead of his usual jovial face, Jeremiah looked deadly serious. "I think it's time we compare notes, Son. It's not every day I get approached by the Secret Service to do the first lady a favor."

Trip looked like he had been punched in the stomach. This was too much. Jeremiah looked confused over Trip's reaction. Senator Cosby was no stranger to insider corruption, and he assumed with Trip's position he was as well. It was obvious by Trip's reaction that Trip was not. John decided it was time to take control.

"Senator," said John. "Let me tell you what we know, and/or suspect, from my investigation and then you tell us what you know, and/or suspect." The senator nodded. "We know that Archibald Industries had a plant

171

open in Kentucky over twenty-five years ago in a small rural town. In that town lived Jason Sparks, Beth George, and David George." The senator looked confused. "These are two new names I uncovered, and they may be at the heart of this entire investigation." Senator Cosby nodded. John continued.

"The parents of Tom Bradley, Amy Jensen, Leroy Jenkins, and Colt McCormick moved their families to Kentucky when the plant opened. Because there were not enough houses in the town where the plant was located, the families all moved to nearby towns in other counties. Most were less than ten miles away from the plant. What we also know is Archibald Staples moved his family into the town where the plant was located. The local pastor, a Brother Jim Walters of Double Forks Southern Missionary Baptist Church, has identified Archibald's daughter as Veronica." John stressed this. He held up the Sunday School picture. "In this picture, the girl the world knows as Lisa Staples, married name Nichols, is identified as Veronica." Chet let out a low whistle. John looked at his friend with a close lipped smile and nodded. He handed Chet the picture. "Chet, I need you to run an age program on this. Age all the children we know in this picture and compare them to how they look today; not just Veronica." Chet looked at him sharply. "I don't want any more surprises. If one of our dead people is someone else, let's find out now."

Chet nodded, took the picture, and started the program. John looked around the room. This was the second time he had told everyone the story and they all looked just as surprised as they did the first time . . . well except for Senator Cosby. This was his first time and there weren't really words for the shock that was on his face. John continued.

"These eight children all attended the same church, and the seven, except for David George, all attended the same Sunday School class. The seven were inseparable all over town. Apparently, David George would tag behind since he was younger than the rest. This went on until around the summer the seven finished their 8th grade year. Apparently, Veronica considered Beth and David her project." John looked at the senator. Jeremiah nodded for John to continue. "David and Beth were raised by their mother . . . well . . . they lived in their mother's house. From what I understand, their mother did next to nothing for them. Veronica tried to," John paused trying to search for the right words.

"Bring them up from their socioeconomic status?" Jeremiah offered. John turned and looked at the senator. Jeremiah smiled. The senator continued. "John, that quote is straight from Lisa Nichols. She wants to help lower socioeconomic families rise above their birth status." Jeremiah huffed. "It's so good to see that pompous, self-inflated, witch thought so highly of herself at such a young age."

John was fighting back the laughter. "So Jeremiah what do you really think about Veronica?" Jeremiah straightened up. He put his weight on his cane and pointed with his other hand.

"Son, that girl thinks the sun don't shine without her say-so. She honestly believes hard working folks can't overcome their surroundings without her or her cronies' help. She believes what she believes so feverously, that if someone were to stand up to her . . . well, I have no idea what she might do to them." Jeremiah's eyes were sparkling. He was on the verge of one of his famous campaign speeches about the power of hard working people. John hated to stop him, but if Jeremiah got going, they would be there all day. John spoke very solemnly.

"Senator Cosby, if what I found is true; it appears she may have already stooped to murder when someone stood up to her." The blood drained from Senator Cosby's face. He turned away from the group. John expected to see disbelief in the senator's eyes, but he didn't. John felt sick to his stomach. The first lady of the United States of America should be above the suspicion of murder, but it appeared that wasn't the case. Jeremiah looked John in the eye.

"John, I wish I could tell you that surprised me, but it doesn't." He paused. "You need to finish your story, because I think, knowing what I know, I have more than enough evidence to move your investigation forward."

Chapter 66

John took a deep breath and continued.

"Sometime that summer, David and Beth George disappeared. The last time either of them has seen was when Brother Walters talked to Beth. Beth confided in Brother Jim that she was gay. Brother Walters told Beth that she could not tell Veronica." Jeremiah grumbled.

"There's a fine how-do-you-do!" Jeremiah exclaimed. "A man of God's worry over this girl was for her not to tell Veronica. What does that tell you about Veronica, or Lisa, or whatever her name was? Let me guess, he was afraid Veronica would do something to Beth because Beth would ruin Veronica's image." John nodded, surprised. "Don't look like that, Boy! I didn't become a senator by not understanding people. So you're talking late 1980's in Kentucky. My guess is Veronica was scared that others would think she was gay by associating with Beth." John nodded.

"That was exactly what Brother Jim said to me," said John. "Anyway, no one has seen the brother and sister since. The group had a meeting place that Bro. Jim and I checked out. There were signs of blood, and a possible struggle. There is a mine shaft that we looked down. There appears to be one body down the hole." John looked at Trip who was just shaking his head. "Anyway, within three weeks from that talk Bro. Jim had with Beth, all of the families of the current murder victims moved back to their original states, and Archibald moved back to Virginia with his daughter, LISA."

Jeremiah was sputtering he was so mad. "Are you telling me that man helped his daughter hide a murder?" John held his hands up.

"Senator, I'm not saying anything. I'm just giving you the facts."

"Oh calm down, John, I'm not mad at you," said Jeremiah. "That man is as dirty as they come, but I can never get anyone to turn over evidence on him." Trip looked up from holding his head in his hands.

"We've opened dozens of cases on Archibald over the years, but nothing ever sticks to him," said Trip. "I've been around long enough to know when someone is dirty, and that guy is as dirty as they come. I had hoped that his daughter was nothing like him, but obviously I was dead wrong." John was looking at Jeremiah. Jeremiah caught the look.

"I'm guessing you would like me to tell you about how the Secret Service met with me last night to try and convince Washington to take you off the case and put my son on it?" Jeremiah loved one upping John, it happened so rarely. John was stunned. "Oh and did I forget I was suppose to nudge my son into taking this case?" John almost leapt into the air. Jeremiah held his hand up before John could speak.

While this was going on, Chet was sitting off to the side pinching his lip; something in the story didn't make sense to him. He began to do a search on Beth George, and Double Forks, Kentucky. Jeremiah continued his conversation while this was going on.

"Unfortunately, John, this agent knew how to say just enough, or not say enough, that I could never pin anything on him. He never specifically said anything about the first lady."

Chet's search came up with no activity. It seems she did disappear around the time John was talking about. Chet decided to search for David George, Double Forks, Kentucky, expecting the same result as Beth. The conversation was continuing behind Chet.

"Trip, we have to send someone to Kentucky to get that body."

Trip shook his head. "John, you do realize if we send forensics down there, it will tip off the first lady." Trip groaned and shook his head. "John, we have a lot of smoke, but very little evidence to pin anything on her. There is one major problem with all of this; do you really think Lisa Nichols killed Jason Sparks, or his four mourners? That's the case you're supposed to be working on, not opening up an over twenty-five year old cold case that may or may not be a murder!"

John was frustrated. Everything Trip said was right. For all the answers he had, there were none that answered the questions in Jessica and Chet's case.

Chet was half listening to what was going on behind him. His mouth had dropped open when the computer returned information on his search. He pulled on Jessica's jacket sleeve. Jessica had been listening to the entire conversation going on in front of her. She turned toward Chet's computer screen. It took her a second to comprehend what she was seeing, but once she did she realized the case hadn't come to a screeching halt like she feared it had.

"Uh . . . guys," she said. John and Trip were going on, ignoring her.

"Trip, you can't just sit back and do nothing . . ." John was interrupted by a shrill whistle. Trip, John, and Senator Cosby turned toward the screen that showed David George's active military file. When John saw the file, it was like a huge lock turned in his head; the tumblers moved and in one instant, John was sure he had figured the case out. He now realized he had a problem if the case was solved. Instead of six murders, he now had six murders and a possible assassination attempt of one of the highest political figures in the US.

Lisa Sparks
Oval Office

Chapter 67

Lisa looked over the Oval Office. Over the next hour she would have her picture made with three of the nation's finest troops. She had cleared out the outer office in spite of the numerous protests. It had taken some doing getting everyone to leave, but few argued with the first lady, especially when the president wasn't around to assist them with Lisa. It would only be her, the cameraman, and two Secret Service agents. Lisa was already thinking about the publicity she could milk this photo-op for. There was a knock on the door behind her. She turned around and saw Agent McDonald.

Lisa sighed to herself. She was going to have to do something about Luke eventually. He was getting a little too close to her, but right now he was needed. She didn't think she would have to take things to the next level to get out of him what she needed, but if she had to, she would. He looked around to make sure they were alone.

"I tried to talk to our mutual friend," said Agent McDonald. Lisa thought Luke had seen one too many Mafia movies. "He wouldn't help us, so I contacted someone to assist us."

Lisa had a concerned look on her face. Luke smiled.

"You're father, Lisa," Luke said. Lisa smiled broadly. She knew deep inside if Luke screwed this up, her father would take care of everything. "I'm going to head out to take care of our friend. The three soldiers are ready.

They all arrived a few minutes ago. I'll get the cameraman and you can get started."

Lisa nodded to Luke and watched him leave. Luke walked out of the Oval Office and through the halls of the White House. Luke was thinking about the first lady. The thoughts he was having about her were wrong. She was married and one of the most powerful women in the world, but part of him really didn't care. He would do anything for her. Luke realized he had walked the halls on autopilot. He kept walking to his destination. He stopped when he reached the lobby where the three soldiers were waiting.

"You two may follow the two Secret Service agents," Luke said to two of the soldiers. They followed the agents leaving Luke alone with David George. David stood up, and reached his hand out to shake Luke's hand.

"Thank you," said David. Luke smiled warmly at him. David continued. "You don't know what this means to me. The first lady has helped shape my life into what it is today and meeting her will mean more to me than you'll ever know." Luke smiled warmly and clapped the soldier on his shoulder.

After Luke walked off, David sat back down and thought to himself, "You have no idea how Lisa has shaped my life. Today I'm gonna make sure she knows exactly how much she shaped it, and so will the entire world."

John Fowler
FBI New York Building

Chapter 68

John stared at the screen in front of him. On the screen, there was an active file on David George. He was alive. That meant that Beth was probably the body down the shaft in Kentucky. His mind was racing through all the scenarios that he could imagine, and they kept coming back to the same conclusion.

Jessica was watching John. She had been quiet all day. What they had shared the night before had put her in a position she had never been in. If she didn't know better, she would say she was falling in love. She saw the look in John's eyes and knew he had solved the case. She had seen that look so many times over the years. John turned and looked at her, catching her glance. He got this dopey lopsided grin on his face. The kind of grin that screamed, "He knew something that you didn't and when he told you, you would feel stupid for not knowing it". Jessica loved that grin. That revelation shocked her. She was surprised by that revelation. It used to make her so mad when he would get it in the past and now . . . she realized how much she had missed him. She found herself grinning back at John. As John kept looking at Jessica, he began barking out orders.

"Chet, I need you to see if David George's unit crossed paths with Jason Spark's unit in Afghanistan." Trip looked at John sharply. Trip closed his eyes as it all began to fall into place. John looked over at the senator. Jeremiah was shaking his head. The look on the senator's face was one of pure shock.

"Boss, I'm also trying to see if he was stateside during Jason's funeral." John nodded. Chet was less than a step behind him in what happened. Chet's fingers were flying across the keyboard as the entire room was quiet waiting to see if what they all suspected was true. Chet quit typing and the room was so silent you could hear a pin drop. John knew what the answers were to the queries Chet had made, but he asked anyway.

"What did you find, Chet?"

"Boss," Chet seemed sick. "Boss, David George found Jason Spark's body in Afghanistan. According to the report, David George killed Jason's killer, a Taliban soldier. David George's tour ended before the funeral of Jason Sparks. The last place I have any information on David is in New York. It's like he fell off the grid after that."

John turned to Trip and Senator Cosby. "Trip, I know you don't want to hear this, but everyone that David George knew from that time in his life is dead but one person."

Trip started to walk around the room muttering. Chet turned back to the keyboard. Something was gnawing at him in the back of his mind. Trip stopped in front of John.

"John, do you realize what you're saying? The last thing we want is to scare the president and first lady with the slim chance there might be someone trying to kill her over something that may or may not have happened over two decades ago!"

John grinned. "Trip, all we're doing is following the case where it takes us. If there is no evidence to back up what we're saying, then we walk away, but if there is evidence, we would not be doing our jobs to let it go." Trip gave John a scouring look. Trip nodded his head in acceptance. John clapped his hands together, excited to get the investigation moving forward.

While this exchange was going on, Chet was staring at the screen again. Jessica happened to turn around at this time and saw what Chet was looking at. She hit him in the shoulder. Chet jerked his head to look at her.

"Chet, is this what I think it is?" Jessica asked. Chet nodded. "GUYS!" John turned and saw what was on the screen. He felt his heart fall into his shoes. Trip's phone began ringing, and so did Senator Cosby's. The color drained from John's face. Trip answered the phone. He said hello and just stood and listened. He hung up and looked at the group.

"There's just been an incident at the White House."

David George
1600 Pennsylvania Avenue-20 Minutes Earlier

Chapter 69

David watched as his two fellow servicemen came back down the hall. The cameraman came up to David and told him he was ready. David stood, smiled, and mentally readied himself. It was time. He walked down the hallway to the exterior office of the Oval Office. David looked around; there were no other visible Secret Service agents except for the two inside the Oval Office. David knew they would be there in seconds, however. The cameraman stepped into the Oval Office and waved David in.

David had thought about his plan for weeks. The most secure room in the White House was the Oval Office. With only two guards he could surprise and overtake, it would just be him, Lisa, and the cameraman in the room; getting her confession. That's all he was after; the confession. He would make Lisa tell the world who she really was and what she had done all those years ago. David smiled. He knew he would die today, but he had been living on borrowed time since he fell down that hole in Kentucky. He had made peace with all he had done. He just wanted justice. Today he would have it.

David stepped into the opening with the agents on either side of him. The first lady was across the room in front of the President's desk with her back to David. David knew it was time. He moved suddenly and without any hesitation. Both his hands sprang outward in a sweeping motion catching the agents in throat. David had been counting on both agents being more at ease with a soldier in the room and not expecting an attack. David spun to his left and grabbed the head of the staggering agent. He brought his right knee up as he shoved the agent's face down. The sick crack of David's knee hitting the agent's skull rang out through the office.

It hadn't even registered yet with the cameraman and the first lady what was happening. David took the gun from the fallen agent's holster. He spun to the other agent. The second agent had grasped his throat and fallen to one knee. He began to realize what was happening and went for his gun. David pistol-whipped him to the ground. He took his gun as well. He sprinted five steps across the room past the cameraman and grabbed the first lady as she turned around. David put the gun to the first lady's head. He spoke to the cameraman.

"Lay down your camera right now and drag the bodies out into the exterior office or I will kill you." Adrenaline shot through the cameraman as he quickly drug the first one out of the room. David nodded toward the second. The cameraman drug him out as well. The cameraman drug the second agent much further out and dove behind a desk in the exterior office. David silently cursed himself. He hurried himself and the first lady across the room and slammed the door to the Oval Office shut. Lisa spoke.

"Do you realize what you have done? Do you know who I am?"

David smiled. "Yes, Veronica, I know exactly who you are. Do you know who I am?"

The blood drained from Lisa's face. She realized, much too late, that she should have taken the note more seriously. For the first time, in a very long time, she was afraid.

Chapter 70

Veronica tried to think who this could possibly be. She had only gotten a glimpse of him earlier. She couldn't place the face or the voice. She tried to muster all of the courage she could. "Who are you?" She asked.

David snorted. "To think Beth thought that you cared about us. That preacher was right; Beth never should have told you her secret."

Veronica's mind was reeling. There was no way this could be Beth's brother. It wasn't possible. He died that day. She knew he did. Veronica thought back. She actually never saw the body. How did he survive? David spoke, like he was reading her mind.

"What's wrong? No quick answer this time, Lisa? No quick ideas like there were when you made Jason think my sister was raping you? I should have done something then, but I was too scared, and then he killed her; the poor idiot. He was just doing what you wanted done, just like the other four. That's why I killed them all fast." Veronica stiffened. "Oh, you didn't know I killed Jason?" David laughed. "Lisa, you should have checked that shaft. I don't know how, but I landed on Beth that day. It saved my life." Veronica felt fear well up in her. She wanted to cry, but she refused to give David the satisfaction. David continued.

"I checked on her immediately. I was no doctor but her neck was all weird. I knew she was dead, and I knew it was all your fault." There was a pounding on the door. David yelled.

"If you come through that door, I will kill her! I'm not kidding!"

A voice came through the other side. "Sir, please keep calm. No one needs to get hurt."

David yelled again. "That's right, and no one will. Now if you want to talk to me it's real simple. There's a

185

phone in here, call it. I only want one thing. I want Lisa here," Veronica stiffened. She felt sick, everything was about to fall apart. She chided herself. Things had already fallen apart. She had to play spin control. David continued. "Sorry about that, but I want Veronica here to confess what happened in Kentucky over twenty-five years ago and then I'll let her go. All I want is a cameraman to tape the confession; none of you Secret Service clowns. I'm not listening to anything else that isn't a phone call!"

David heard a mumbled ok from the other side and then it was quiet. Veronica knew she needed to do something to get David off of his game. She went with a desperation plan.

"You know they already have someone close solving the case," said Veronica.

"Oh really?" replied David.

"Oh yes. They pulled some guy out of retirement. He grew up in Kentucky. Who knows, we may have known him. He's already talked to Tom's family. It's only a matter of time before he puts together what happened. David I didn't do anything that day; it was Jason."

David was very quiet. He was considering what Lisa was saying. He knew everything Lisa said was about gaining an advantage.

"So you think he knows everything?" David asked. Veronica nodded, very sure of herself. "What is his name?" The question caught Veronica off guard and David knew she was trying to throw him off his game. He had turned the tables and now he knew exactly what to do. He tightened his grip on her and buried the gun a little further into her. "What? Is? His? Name?!" Veronica realized she had been outmaneuvered. The pain was getting to her.

"John! John Fowler!" David eased his grip on her.

With that, the phone rang. He motioned for Lisa to hand it to him. He dodged as she tried to swing at him with

186

it and subdued her. He put the phone between his neck and shoulder. He made sure he had a firm grip on Lisa with one hand, and in the other hand he had the gun pointed into her ribs.

"Listen," said David. "I know you are going to try and wait me out. I'll make this very simple. I want former FBI agent John Fowler to film Lisa's . . . I mean VERONICA's confession. Afterwards, I give myself up and let both people go unhurt. You have three hours or I kill her." David hung up the phone and looked down at Lisa. Lisa finally broke and started to cry.

"That's good. That's real good," said David. "Before today is done, you are going to cry every tear you have stored up in your miserable body."

Chapter 71

Trip was having trouble breathing. This was more than he ever dreamed he would have to deal with in all his years at the FBI. He was in the New York office, not the DC office. Yet here he was, smack in the middle of a hostage situation. This wasn't any hostage though; this was the first lady of the United States of America. He was jolted back to reality with a smack across his face by Senator Cosby.

"Boy!" Senator Cosby was shaking him now. "Trip!" Trip waved his hand that he was alright. "Good gracious man, you're supposed to be in charge here. Act like a man!" John was trying very hard not to crack up at everything that was going on. He had no idea what had happened at the White House, but this was a scene like he had never seen.

Trip turned to John. "They need you in Washington, D.C."

John was confused. "What are you talking about Trip? What is going on?"

"Someone has managed to take Veronica Staples hostage," said Trip. "The perpetrator has said he wants a cameraman." Trip looked directly at John. "John, you are the only one he will let run the camera."

"No!" Jessica exclaimed. The whole group turned as one to look at her. Jessica looked more shocked than any of them. She covered her mouth with her hands. Trip groaned and rolled his eyes. Chet looked very uncomfortable. Senator patted John on the back, knowingly. As for John . . . John rocked back on his heels. He straightened his tie. John's eyes were dancing and he had the self-assured half-cocked grin on his face that Jessica didn't know if she wanted to smack off or kiss off.

"Let's give these two a moment," said the senator.

"A moment!" Trip exclaimed. "Senator, do you realize the first lady of the United States of America is currently a hostage?!"

Senator Cosby drew himself up. "Son, I sure do. And do I have a shock for you . . . I don't care! Do you realize what these two kids have been through over the years?" Jeremiah was in rare form. "I don't really care if David George blows that Staples girl's brains all over the Oval Office! These two have something they need to do or say, or whatever! I'm sure John here understands the urgency and won't take one second more than needed, but I'm also sure he won't leave one second earlier than he needs to!"

John didn't know what to say. Trip looked at John and Jessica, squared his jaw, and nodded.

"C'mon, Chet!" Trip barked. Chet hightailed it out of the room with Trip following. Senator Cosby walked to the door and gave John the thumbs up. John smiled and turned toward Jessica. His face met her hand and a smack rang out through the foxhole. John thought his jaw had become unhinged. He looked at Jessica, saw the anger on her face, and realized this was going to take a few more minutes than he originally thought.

Chapter 72

"What have you done to me?" Jessica screamed at John. John was beyond confused.

In John's defense, he didn't have a lot of experience in the world of women and being single. His relationship with Sam was different than most. The two of them had hit it off immediately and didn't play a lot of the games men and women play. John was thinking about answering that he didn't move his face in time for her hand to hit it, but thought better of it. Jessica started up again.

"I used to be in control of my feelings. I use to be stoic and able to hide any feeling I had for anything on this job! For crying out loud John, I haven't seen you in three years! The last time I saw you I knew you hated me, and it didn't make me blink. You don't get to make me feel this way! You don't!" She was pacing now and John stood back letting her get it all out. "I told my boss . . . no, wait, no. I screamed at my boss, NO! Why? Because of you; the man who has made it his life's personal mission to drive me crazy?"

John thought it might be time to reply, but something in his mind from his married days told him to just shut up and listen. It was probably the right call, as Jessica continued on with her diatribe.

"You." Jessica stopped. She walked right up to him until there was barely room for sunlight between them. She pointed her finger and poked it in his chest. "You, are supposed to be helping me save my career, not helping me destroy it. You arrogant, self-important, narcissistic . . ."

John knew what was coming next. There would be a bunch of adjectives used to describe him that John really didn't care for. John couldn't help thinking how hot she looked when she was angry. In one motion, right in the midst of her calling him names, he grabbed her by the head and kissed her.

Jessica was taken aback by the kiss, but she quickly responded by kissing him back. The kiss caused her to curl her toes to the point she heard them crack. John broke the kiss.

Jessica was left breathless. She thought about grabbing him and throwing him on the desk but decided that would probably not be appropriate given the whole hostage situation going on right now. She couldn't let him think he had won though. She gathered herself, and spoke quietly.

"So I say all of those nasty things about you," she began. She was considering just kissing him again, but she knew she shouldn't. She took a deep breath. "I say all of those things about you, and your response is to kiss me?"

John had shocked himself with what he had just done. He knew he should be on a helicopter or plane to DC right now, but that was the furthest thing on his mind. Right now the only thing on his mind was Jessica, and he really was considering telling her.

"It seemed like the thing to do," replied John. His eyes were dancing and she was losing herself in them. Jessica wondered what he might do if she called him worse. For a second she let her mind get carried away. She shook her head to bring her back to the moment before she did something that would get them both fired.

"Well, it was a response I wasn't suspecting," she said.

John smiled. He kissed the end of her nose and tried to turn to leave. It was then he noticed that she had both her hands gripping his jacket. John looked at her and Jessica smiled sheepishly.

"The senator said you should not leave one moment before you needed to," Jessica reminded him coyly.

"Jessica, if I don't leave right now, I'm not going to leave and the first lady will die," John said. "That's not the kind of pressure most relationships can handle." Jessica was taken aback with this revelation about them.

"We have a relationship?" Jessica asked. John took her hands in his.

"Don't we?" He asked softly. Jessica thought she might start calling him names; then she thought about throwing him on the desk. Jessica was getting lost in her thoughts when John cupped his index finger under her chin and lifted her head until she was looking straight into his eyes. Jessica felt her knees buckle. John put his finger on her lips and slowly backed away. When he had backed away as far as he could without breaking contact, he turned and started to leave the room. He stopped at the doorway and turned to face her.

"I'll be back in a little while," he said. Jessica didn't dare open her mouth for fear of what she might say. She held onto the desk with one hand so she wouldn't chase after him. She waved to him. John tipped his hat and walked out of the foxhole. Jessica stood there for a minute not sure what to do. She finally let out a long sigh.

"Sam, you were right, he's something else . . . and worst of all, he knows it!" She said out loud. "I hope it's okay, Sam. I hope it's okay, whatever he and I have." Jessica could swear she felt the arm of her friend around her in support.

Chapter 73

John headed up the elevator; his hearting beating so hard he thought it would burst. He had to do something about Jessica. Good grief, could she push all of his buttons. He thought to himself for a minute that it might not be such a bad thing. He almost bolted back to the foxhole. He shook his head to clear it. He needed to concentrate on what was going on. He had been alone for three years; another day wasn't going to kill him. The elevator stopped at Trip's floor and the doors opened. Trip and Senator Cosby were waiting on him. They joined him in the elevator as it headed toward the roof.

There was very little to talk about in the elevator. Trip looked very uncomfortable. John was whistling an eighties tune. When he came to a line that Trip recognized, Trip groaned.

"Really?" Trip asked, with a pained expression on his face. "Don't you know anything from this decade or even last?" Jeremiah chuckled.

"Don't be too hard on him, Son," said Jeremiah. "If I were him with that pretty young thing, I'd be singing something by Ole Blue Eyes himself. Loudly, and badly out of tune!"

John chuckled. Trip turned to Jeremiah.

"And you're okay with those two?" Trip asked. "I mean, Jeremiah, Sam seemed to be like a daughter to you. I would say she probably meant more to you than your actual son."

Jeremiah drew himself up. "Lionel Pennyworth Smothers III, I will have you know that girl still means more to me than my own son! He was born with the belief he deserved everything that was ever given to him and that ever could be given to him!" Jeremiah turned to John. "Son, did you have any idea how wealthy that girl was when you met her?" John shook his head no. Jeremiah's eyes were fierce. He spoke very angrily. "I wish my boy was a tenth of the person Samantha was. And that's another thing! When this is over, you two owe that girl some justice! You hear me?" Jeremiah was very worked up. John filed this outburst in his head for the future. Something was up here, but now was not the time to deal with it. Trip turned to Jeremiah. He looked rather irate. Trip spoke very softly.

"You're exactly right." Both Jeremiah and John could have fallen over. "We have done Samantha Fowler a huge disservice by not finding her killer. When this is over, sir, we will rectify that situation." Jeremiah was a little taken aback.

"Well," Jeremiah was a little unsure of his words. "Good. As for Jessica, Samantha loved her like a sister. Did you know, John, that young lady kept me abreast of what was going on in Sam's investigation for the last three years?" The look on John's face answered that question. "That girl deserves happiness, and if it's with this fine, young man . . . by God, that's alright with me!"

The elevator stopped at the roof. The door opened. Jeremiah and Trip exited the elevator. They both turned to see what was holding up John. John knew. It finally all fit together. He looked Trip dead in the eye. Trip gulped.

"That's what has Jessica and Chet in trouble isn't it?" Trip tried to make like he didn't understand. John ignored Trip. He walked out of the elevator past Trip and Jeremiah. It was clear by the look on Jeremiah's face that he also knew what John had just put together. That made complete sense.

"My little explosion at Arthur at the funeral. . ." John looked at Trip and knew he was right on the money. "Arthur demanded to find out who Sam's killer was. They couldn't solve the case; for whatever reason. That's why getting me back for this case could save their careers. If I could solve this, everyone thought that I would jump on Sam's case and that would make Arthur back off."

Both Jeremiah and Trip looked sheepish. Jeremiah began to chuckle. Trip looked at him and began to laugh. Jeremiah spoke.

"Arthur was right; he is the best detective I've ever seen. He's almost right on this." John was confused. "I went to Arthur to get him to lay off of Washington about Jessica and Chet. He agreed to if you would come back for one more case and we offered you Sam's case. If you don't take it, Sam and Chet are okay. Arthur believes whoever killed Sam wants you dead. If you were in the open and publicly working again, it would draw out Sam's killer. That hasn't happened. Trip and I have already gotten Arthur to promise that he will not approach the people at Washington again. John, I honestly think Arthur would have been happy if the killer had just shown up and shot you." John laughed.

"Gone three years," Trip said shaking his head. "Gone three years and you figured this and the quadruple homicide out in less than a week. John . . . John, I've missed you and the FBI has missed you."

John looked out over the city from the top of the building. He had to admit he missed this. He was good at what he did. Not only was he good, he enjoyed it. That's why Sam never had a problem with the danger involved in his job. John loved cracking cases and puzzles. John knew however this ended it would be hard for him not to come back. Trip came up beside him and gestured to the helicopter. They boarded the helicopter and took off.

"Can we make it in time?" John asked.

"It's about 250 miles to DC and we can go around 130 mph. We should have time to spare," answered Trip. John sat back and wondered what he would do once inside the room with David George.

Luke McDonald
1600 Pennsylvania Ave

Chapter 74

Things had gone from bad to worse in Luke's opinion. There was a command post set-up outside the White House with hostage negotiators talking to David George. News vans were on one side of the command center. The men that Luke had been sent were sitting in a van away from all the chaos. It was actually the perfect spot to take Senator Cosby, but there was no sense doing so now. Lisa was going down and there was nothing he could do to help her. Luke's phone rang.

"This is Luke."

"You know who this is. I have it confirmed that Senator Cosby is approaching your site via helicopter. He will be arriving with agents John Fowler and Trip. You need to separate Cosby from them."

Luke was stunned. "Begging your pardon, sir, but what is the point? Lisa has been taken and whatever secret she was trying to keep hidden is about to be exposed."

"Listen to me," said the voice on the other end of the line. "We can use the senator as leverage. Right now I need every advantage I can get to help her. We can use the senator to blackmail his son if we need to. A FBI agent on my side would go a long way toward helping me. Keep in mind that Senator Cosby could possibly win a Presidential election and that would be bad for me. This is my chance to help myself and my family. Remember, Son, I have a lot of influence over her and if I decided that you are best for her, she will listen to me. You would like that wouldn't you?"

Luke was smiling broadly. "Yes. Yes, sir, I would. I'll take care of everything."

Luke could hear the chopper beginning to land.

"They are on their way now, sir. Is there anything else?"

"No. Take care of this for me, and I won't forget it." Luke hung up and smiled. In a little while, he would get what he had always wanted.

Chapter 75

The helicopter landed and John, Trip and Senator Cosby disembarked. Luke ran up to the group. Senator Cosby looked on in disdain.

"Senator, I know we've had our disagreements, but there is a life at stake. Someone would like to see you. He has a few ideas." Jeremiah snorted but nodded.

"Give me and John a minute," Jeremiah said. Luke nodded and moved away. Cosby grabbed John's arm.

"Son, if you get a chance to make her story public, you need to. You cannot let that girl get away with what she has done. Do you understand?" John nodded. Jeremiah was very insistent. "I blame myself. If I had run for President, I would have beaten that fool, but I didn't want to get into it with Lisa's father. That man is dangerous son. Don't forget that. He probably has fourteen contingency plans. I'm sure that is who wants to see me right now. Take care of yourself, ma'boy. That woman is not worth you getting killed over."

Senator Cosby clapped John on the shoulder and followed Luke. Secret Service hurried John over to the command post. Luke and Senator Cosby walked over to the far parking lot that was deserted except for the black van. They walked up beside it, and Luke stopped. Cosby was beside the van with Luke standing beside him. The van door slid opened and Cosby was grabbed. A cloth was pressed against his face. Cosby struggled for a second and went limp. Luke looked around to see if anyone was watching. No one had looked in their direction. The four men in the van were wearing masks. One held up a stun gun in one hand and the cloth in the other.

"Oh, come on," said Luke. "Please give me the cloth!" The man in the mask shook his head no and hit Luke with the stun gun. Luke flopped like a fish out of water. After he was out, the man in the mask drug Luke behind some shrubbery and left him. The man climbed back into the van, shut the door, and the van took off away from the grounds.

Chapter 76

The Secret Service pulled John into the command post. They were barking orders at him. Apparently they had cut the time a little close. Different agents were screaming at him. "No heroics!" "Do what he says!" "Protect the first lady!"

John's head was spinning. He had about had it with all of these orders. Trip saw the look in John's eyes and tried to cross the room quickly to stop him. John picked up the red phone that connected directly to David George. Everyone in the room froze. John smiled.

"David, this is John Fowler. Look, I just got here. I am going to go get a quick lesson in how to use this video camera and I'm going to come in there. Is there any food or anything I can bring you?" John listened to the voice on the other end. "Well, David, we can use the camera in there, but are you sure it's not broken, because I'm not. I don't know how to fix one if it is, so may I please bring in this camera? It's not a trick, David; I'm trying to do exactly as you ask. If I do as you ask, you'll do what you promised, right?" There was a pause. Everyone in the room held their breath. John gave a big smile, and the room exhaled. "I'll see you very soon, David, and we'll end this."

John hung up. Before he could turn around, there was someone in his face getting ready to yell. John beat him to it.

"Back off!" Everyone was silent. "Now I don't know what has been said about me before I got here, so let me hit all the highlights. Yes, I am a recovering alcoholic. I have been sober for three years. No, I do not have a death wish. No, I'm not going to do what you tell me to do. I'll handle this my way. That is, I will walk out of there with both the first lady and David George alive. Any other option is non-negotiable. Are we all clear?" Trip smiled a tight-lipped smile. There was grumbling, but no one disagreed. "Now, where is a news crew so I can learn how to be the world's greatest cameraman in less than five minutes?"

Chapter 77

John walked up to a national news crew. The reporter there recognized him from John's work years before. John stuck his hand out.

"Hi, I'm John Fowler. I'm about to make you an offer you can't refuse. I need to borrow one of your cameras. I need you to show me how to use it."

Sheila Lane had been covering events like this for years, but she had never had this happen before. She extended her hand and shook John's.

"Sheila Lane. I talked to you before during the Mafia bust." John blushed.

"I'm sorry. I was probably drunk and said something inappropriate."

"You probably were and you did. I don't think what you suggested was humanly possible." John dropped his head. He sighed and then raised his head. Sheila was smiling at him.

"Your partner spoke to me at length afterwards." John looked confused. "Jessica, I believe was her name." John was taken aback; how long had Jess been covering for him? "Anyway, she told me about your wife and the whole deal. I'm really sorry."

"Thank you," said John. "Now, I quickly need you to teach me how to use your news camera." Sheila waved over her cameraman and he gave John an extensive lesson. The last thing he showed John was a switch on the back that activated a red light.

"Now make sure to have the switch off," said the cameraman. "If the light is off, it records only to the camera. If the switch is on and this light is red, it would send us the feed out here in the truck."

"Oh really?" said John. John turned toward Sheila with a mischievous grin on his face. "Sheila, as a journalist, what would you do if you were to receive that feed?"

Sheila raised an eyebrow. "Well, John, as a journalist, it would be my duty to send the feed national. In other words, it would be on TV as quick as the signal could hit the relays."

"Huh," said John. "I would have thought that Secret Service would cut it off or something."

"If the feed went out during whatever might be happening, there would be a public outcry. Besides I don't think anyone would mind seeing the first lady being taken down a peg."

John nodded. "Well, I'll just have to make sure that switch doesn't light up the little red light now won't I?"

Sheila nodded. John smiled and started toward the command post. John called back.

"Hey, Sheila, do you think you'd get an award for that?"

Sheila smiled, "Oh, yeah." John smiled and continued on.

Chapter 78

As John headed down the deserted halls of the White House, he had to admit he was a little excited. He was about to solve an "unsolvable case" and solve an over twenty-five year old case that hadn't even been opened yet! Man, it was hard being that good! John chuckled to himself. He deserved many of those names that Jessica liked to call him.

He reached the door to the outer office to the Oval Office. The agent in charge radioed to the command center to let them know John was there. The command center called in to David George. John waited patiently to be told to enter. He didn't want to do a thing to spook David.

"John Fowler!" David yelled. "You may come in. If anyone else follows, or if you are armed, I kill the first lady and then you!"

"I'm coming alone, David," yelled John. John slowly opened the door to the outer office and looked in. He saw no one and slowly walked in. After he stepped in he closed the door behind him. "David, I'm in the outer office, by myself. Please don't shoot me." John slowly walked to the inner office. "David, I'm at the door, what would you like me to do?"

"Open the door, very slowly," said David. "I will kill her if you try anything."

"David," said John. "You have nothing to worry about, I'm just gonna open the door. I have only the camera in my hands, and there is no gun anywhere on me." John opened the door very carefully. He slowly walked through. He saw a man with a gun pointed toward the first lady's head. John came in, and shut door behind him. John laid the camera on the chair and stepped away from it.

"What are you doing?" David asked.

"I thought you might want to examine the camera and make sure it's exactly what I said it was." John held his hands up. David chuckled.

"I trust you, sir. If you do anything what-so-ever, I'm simply going to put a bullet through the first lady here, understand?"

"I sure do, sir," said John. John slowly walked up to the camera, examined and flipped a switch on the back. The red light came on.

"Whoa," said David. "What is that light?"

"Sir, this building is very secure; I need to record everything on this camera. The red light means it's not transmitting but recording to the camera. When this is all over, I take it to the network and the world finds out your story."

David looked upset. "So, you can't transmit live?"

"No, sir, I'm afraid you can't," John replied. Lisa smiled, she knew she could say exactly what David wanted to hear, and it would never air. The Secret Service would take care of that. David George would go to jail for murder and she would go on being first lady. The downside was John Fowler would be a hero and Senator Cosby would find a way to use that to his advantage, but her father already had a contingency plan in place for that. It was going to be a great day.

"Okay," David said. "What do you want me to do?"

"Boss, you're the one with the gun," said John. "Last time I checked that meant you got to make all the rules."

David smiled and nodded. "We're going to get on just fine," said David.

John looked back to make sure that the red light was on. He saw Lisa smile when he fed her the line about the camera not being able to transmit. Lisa would now tell the truth, which would keep David from killing her, but would also ensure she would pay for what happened to Beth all those years ago. Bro. Jim, this is for you.

Chapter 79
Outside in the News Truck

Pete was sitting at his spot in the news truck watching the feeds come in. He stared at one monitor and couldn't believe what he was seeing. He ran to the door and shouted out.

"Sheila!" He yelled. "Who has camera 6?'

Trip had wandered outside of command central. He didn't trust John to do things by the book. He knew that John had another agenda, and John would do whatever it took to get that done. He heard Pete yelling from the news truck, and Trip knew where he could keep tabs on John. He ran over as Sheila approached the truck. Trip pulled out his FBI credentials. Pete stood there like a statue. Trip turned to Sheila.

"Look, that is my agent in there," began Trip. "Actually he's not an agent any longer, he's just a consultant. Either way, he's my friend, and I need to see what he's up to. It could be he's trying to send me a message, and if I can't hear or see what's going on, I won't know how to help him. I promise you I have no plans of shutting down anything."

Sheila didn't like it, but there was a lot of sense in what Trip said. She wondered how John was going to pull all of this off by himself. She motioned Pete out of the way and they both went inside. Trip smiled when he saw the monitor. John had gone live. He was going to take down Lisa, or Veronica, or whatever the heck her name was. He turned to Sheila.

"Is this feed being broadcast out to the country right now?" Trip asked.

Sheila was stunned. "You're telling me to broadcast this?"

Trip shook his head no. "I'm telling you I won't shut it down. You might want to bar that door if you decide to do it."

Sheila turned to Pete, who took off. He locked the door and began to pile stuff in front of it. Sheila got on the phone and began talking. Trip watched the TV broadcast on another monitor. An anchor was on TV talking about the situation in the White House. He looked confused for a split second and then Trip was watching Lisa, John, and the man he could only assume was David George.

"Ok, John," he said to no one. "Bring this one home. And make sure you bring yourself home alive."

Chapter 80

John held the camera where David's and Lisa's faces were perfectly framed. "Not bad," he thought.

"Anytime you're ready, David, I'm sure Lisa is about ready to end all of this," said John.

"First of all," began David. "Her name is Veronica. She came to my home town in Kentucky when I was a young boy. She took an interest in me and my sister, Beth. Our mom was a drunk and we had no idea who our dad was, or if we had the same father. Beth took care of me like she was my mom."

John had heard the majority of this story, but he wanted to make sure he got every bit of this broadcasted so people would know exactly who and what Lisa was. David continued.

"Anyway, Veronica here used to come around and do things with us. She helped Beth in school and gave her hand-me-down clothes that were much better than anything we owned. To tell you the truth, I didn't think some of them had ever been worn." Lisa scoffed.

"They weren't hand-me-downs you idiot," Lisa said. "They were new, or clothes I had never worn. I swear you are still the trash I thought you were twenty-five years ago! You and your sister were, and still are, beneath me! Why did I ever try and help the two of you? You both ruined my life!" Lisa gasped as the gun was being dug into her ribs. John acted quickly.

"David," he warned. "Don't do it man. You are getting exactly what you want out of her. You want everyone to see exactly who she is and what she's done to you and your sister. You need to let her say whatever it is she's going to say."

David nodded. He relaxed his grip. "I apologize, Veronica, feel free to say whatever you feel is appropriate." Veronica shot David a death look.

"You really are an idiot," said Veronica. "You do realize that when this is over you will spend the rest of your life in prison."

"I may," replied David. "But I will finally have justice for you murdering my sister just because you were afraid someone would think you were gay! You won't be the first lady anymore, and there is nothing that you or your father can do to fix it!"

Chapter 81

Lisa was furious. "You have no proof of that!" She exclaimed. John felt he was about to lose control of the situation . . . if he ever had control to start with.

"Lisa, calm down," said John. Lisa glared at him. Was it because he didn't refer to her as the first lady or Mrs. Nichols? John really didn't care. He really hoped she didn't push his buttons too far or he was afraid he'd let David shoot her.

"Lisa, why don't you simply tell what happened in the cave that day." Lisa nodded.

"I had gone to meet Jason Sparks that day," Lisa began. "You know, the Captain that was killed in Afghanistan?" John nodded. "The one that just happened to run into David while they were stationed there and ended up dead?" She asked the question accusingly at David. John started to get a sinking feeling in his gut that Lisa was doing something she hadn't planned on. David had never responded to any of Lisa's accusations, but worse than that, there was no actual proof of David killing anyone. Lisa was actually starting the basis for an insanity defense. A lawyer could say that David saw Jason killed in Afghanistan and it triggered all of his memories or some craziness like that. John thought about stopping her, but decided against it. Lisa continued.

"I was there to see Jason when Beth showed up. Jason hadn't gotten there yet. Beth told me that she was gay, and that she wanted me. She attacked me. She grabbed my breast and put her hand over my mouth so no one could hear." That was strange, thought John. Why, deep in a cave, would you cover someone's mouth? No one should hear any shouts down there. That statement was really bothering John, but it was bothering David even more. John realized what was happening but was powerless to stop it; even if he wanted to. John was afraid it was going to come down to physical threats to learn the truth, and it seemed he was right. David shoved the gun back into Lisa's ribs.

"Do you really think I'm a fool?" David was furious. "Veronica, tell the truth now, or so help me God I will kill you right here and now!"

Chapter 82

John didn't move. Honestly, there was nothing he could do to stop it. Lisa looked to John for help, but John just kept the camera pointed on her.

"Okay! Okay!" Lisa was sobbing. "Beth told me she was gay. I was . . . Don't make me do this, David." Lisa was begging now. David moved the gun and Lisa gasped. "Okay, you've got to remember this was the late 1980's. It was Kentucky, and people were homophobic. Many just assumed if you had a friend that was a certain way, then you were as well. I didn't just want to be the President, I dreamed of being President. Beth ended my hope that day. I wanted to be the first woman President of the United States and I couldn't have anything that could be questioned on my record."

Lisa looked at the ground. John couldn't decide if she was near tears because of what happened, or because she was sorry she got caught. Lisa looked up and continued.

"So when Beth told me . . . I knew Jason was in the next room." Lisa paused, and John was pretty sure what happened next. "I yelled out that I was being attacked. I grabbed both of Beth's hands. I put one on my breast." John was right . . . he was hoping he was wrong. He was hoping that Lisa wasn't this despicable of a person, but he was wrong. Lisa continued. "I took my other hand, put it around her wrist and put her hand over my mouth like she was trying to quiet me. That's when Jason ran in."

John was barely breathing he was listening so closely. He was positive that Lisa didn't physically kill Beth, but she was definitely the mastermind behind Beth's death. Lisa took a deep breath and continued.

"Jason grabbed a rock and hit her in the back of the head with it. I'm pretty sure it killed her instantly. Anyway, Jason took Beth and threw her into the boards that

213

were covering the mine shaft." David dug the gun into Lisa's ribs. John started to move, but Lisa put a hand out to stop him. "Jason did it off of my suggestion. It was an accident and we were kids. The truth is I never killed anyone. Jason Sparks killed Beth, and then tried to kill David." John about dropped the camera with that revelation.

Chapter 83

John regained his composure after that last nugget of information. He looked at David who nodded. Lisa continued her story.

"About that time, David, who was a couple of years younger than us, attacked Jason. It all went crazy then. Our friends showed up. I told them that Beth had tried to rape me and they tried to comfort me. While that was going on, Jason and David fought. I saw Jason shove David. I don't think Jason knew where David was standing because he pushed him through the opening in the boards and down the hole." John couldn't believe what he was hearing.

"I landed on my sister's body," David said softly. "Her neck was at a real weird angle, and I was sure she was dead." David was quiet for a second. John thought, for just a second, he saw the face of the scared little boy who had just seen his sister die and had almost been killed himself. Then, the softness was gone from David's face and the sternness of the young man who had grown up with the solemn vow to get vengeance for his sister's death returned. When he spoke, it was with confidence.

"After making sure nothing was too badly hurt I made my way through some tunnels and came out an opening in the cave that was away from town. I headed up into the hills just wanting to get away from Veronica and the Staples. I knew it would all be covered up. I had dealt with Veronica for the past few years and I knew she always got what she wanted. An old couple raised me until I turned 18 and joined the armed forces. I had basically put it all out of my mind until I saw Jason Sparks in Afghanistan."

"You mean until you killed him and then killed our other four friends at his funeral!" Lisa was furious. John decided it would be a good time to step in before things got completely out of hand.

"Well, it's nice to finally see a FBI case have nothing to do with aliens or UFOs," said John. Both David and Lisa looked at John like he was crazy. John had to admit it was kinda funny given the circumstances. He just hoped the right person heard what he had just said.

Trip
In the News Truck

Chapter 84

Trip heard what John said and smiled to himself. He had to admit they had one of the strangest code lines, but they both knew exactly what he meant.

"Sheila, thank you for letting me watch this. Remember when I said I might have to help my agent? That time is right now. I need you to let me out of here." Sheila looked at Trip. She saw the seriousness on his face. She nodded to her partner and he began to move the barriers from the door. Trip got out of the truck and ran over to the command post. He didn't waste any time going through proper protocols. He noticed that everyone was watching the news feed.

"I don't know who is in charge in here, but I am John Fowler's supervisor, and that was our code phrase he just uttered. I need in there now!" Three different people started to object. Trip didn't play around. "Listen to me very carefully. I know what each code he uses means and we don't have the time to teach you guys." That was a lie, but everyone in the room didn't need to know that. "I'm going in there with or without your help! Now, are you going to help me and my agent?"

Less than a minute later Trip was working his way through the White House. At each checkpoint agents were aware of his coming and showed him where to go next. Trip got to the outer office of the Oval office. The agent in charge there was simply waiting on Trip's command.

"Here's what's going to happen," said Trip. "I'm going in this door and leave it open a crack. When you hear me call out that it is all clear, you come in. The only time you get to disregard that command is if you hear a shot coming from inside of that office. Are we clear, gentlemen?" Trip looked around and the team all nodded in agreement. It didn't matter what agency or branch of government, most of these agents understood one thing, a command. Trip took a deep breath and opened the door to the outer office. He made his way through until he was right beside the door to the inner office. He waited. It was all up to John now as to when the move was to be made. Trip just hoped no one got hurt.

John
Oval Office

Chapter 85

John had said the phrase. He knew he had to give Trip a minimum of five minutes, if not ten to get into position. There was only so long he thought he could keep David from shooting Lisa. There was only so long he thought he could convince himself David shouldn't shoot Lisa. John spoke to try to break the tension.

"So Jason killed Beth and tried to kill David. What about their mother? Why didn't she report them missing?" David's eyes flashed and for a second John thought he had made a big mistake. Contempt for John covered Lisa's face. Oh well, thought John, she's not the first woman to hate me. Lisa almost spat out the words.

"That piece of trash! When I told her what happened to her children and suggested she shouldn't go to the police because they might arrest her for neglect, she basically traded her silence for $10,000.00." John felt sick to his stomach. What kind of evil girl was Lisa? Lisa kept on.

"I then made suggestions to Daddy that I didn't like the kids here and that they should be sent away. I also told him that I would like to change my name and have nothing to do with that cesspool of a town. Daddy agreed after I convinced him that everyone had been mean to me. Daddy sent all of the kid's parents back to their original states. He gave them raises so it wouldn't look suspicious. I asked him for $10,000.00 to give to Mrs. George to help out with her kids after we left. I told him we needed to help those less fortunate than us."

She saw the look on John's face. It was one of disdain. That was fine by Lisa. She had protected her father from any possible fallout. She knew the tape would never get out, but John knew Senator Cosby and John might let Cosby know what was said here. The last thing she wanted to do was give Senator Cosby any kind of idea to look into her father's past.

John was revolted by what he had heard. He looked at David. David almost had a look on his face that said, "And you thought I was bad?" Lisa was evil in John's book. Not just evil, but despicable. John had to hold his face steady and not smile. He was about to bring down the wickedest person he'd ever met and he didn't want to tip his hand.

"Is there anything else either of you think needs to be told?" John asked.

"I think the world has heard everything I wanted them to." David replied. David let Lisa go. He walked over to a chair near John holding the gun by its barrel. He laid the gun on the chair, stepped back several steps, got down on his knees and put his hands behind his head with his fingers interlocking.

John picked up the gun and placed the camera on the desk still pointing toward Lisa and David. Lisa stayed away from David. John walked between them just in case Lisa decided to kick David in the ribs or something. John faced Lisa.

"Lisa," began John. "What I'd like to say to you is . . . You have the right to remain silent, however I'm not a current agent," as John was speaking he was walking across the room to open the door to the inner office. There was Trip with his handcuffs out. He crossed the room and began to put the cuffs on Lisa. John continued. "And since I'm not, I'll just have to watch Trip arrest you and settle for that."

220

Trip shouted all clear and began to read Lisa her rights. The Secret Service and FBI agents flooded the office. One agent cuffed David and whispered to him that he deserved a medal. The agents read David his rights as they walked him away. David mouthed the words, "Thank you" to John as they took him off. Trip was still reading Lisa her rights. John spoke.

"So this whole thing," John began by waving his hand at the oval office. "This whole thing happened just so you could become the President, and when that didn't work out, you decided the next best thing you could do was be the first lady? Is that about right, Lisa?" Lisa didn't say a word, obviously invoking her right to remain silent.

Trip had finished reading Lisa her rights and shook his head, amused with John's questioning.

"Really, John?" Trip asked. "You think she's going to admit that someone didn't do exactly what she wanted? You think she was going to allow someone who wasn't on her level of society take her down?" Trip was looking at Lisa disgustedly as he spoke. "This woman would never admit that someone she felt was below her station in life could affect her."

One of the agents standing beside the two of them shook his head at John and Trip's conversation.

"You realize you two just took down the first lady of the United States of America and you're trying to get her to incriminate herself?" The agent asked. John and Trip looked at each other and nodded.

"Yeah that's about right," said Trip.

"We're just trying to save the American people some money on a trial," said John with a smile. Trip groaned.

"I think you have all the incriminating evidence you need," said the agent.

Lisa was listening to the exchange, but the last comment by the agent bothered her. She had taken all she could stand and had one of her famous Lisa Nichols outbursts.

"You have got to be kidding me!" Lisa screamed. Trip and John turned slowly with huge grins on their faces to face the first lady. "You idiots have arrested me! How?"

John smiled and walked over to President's desk and brought back the camera. He pointed to the red light on the end of the camera. Lisa shrugged her shoulders to say, "So?"

"Lisa. Sweetie," began John. Lisa was glaring at him. "I lied. The red light means that we are transmitting live." Lisa's face fell. The smile fell off of John's face. He was deadly serious. "You see, ma'am, I'm a Kentucky boy myself. I've seen many of those . . . what was the phrase again?" John asked Trip.

"Pieces of trash," replied Trip helpfully.

"Ah, yes," said John. "I've seen many of those 'pieces of trash'," John said using air quotes. "Make their lives out to be so much better without the help of condescending brats like you." Lisa was turning red and making strangling noises. John ignored her and continued. "When I had put enough together and found out that David had you hostage, I just had to find a way to get you to tell what really happened." John moved in really close and spoke quietly where only Trip and Lisa could hear him. "But you see, part of your story just doesn't jive with me, if you know what I mean. I don't think your daddy is quite as innocent as you would like me to believe he is." John turned to Trip as he said that.

Trip put his left arm across his chest to support his right arm. With his right arm he was tapping his finger

222

against his lip. He had a "hmm" face as he did this. He lowered his hand and turned to John.

"Do you think we should open a file on Mr. Archibald Staples?" Trip asked.

"I think he has to be considered at least as a person of interest, don't you, Veronica?" John said her name with contempt. The color drained from Lisa's face. She tried to keep her composure. She responded with four simple words.

"I want my lawyer." Trip turned to the other agents.

"Get her out of here," said Trip. He turned and saw a man in a suit enter the room. "Aw, crap." John turned to see what had Trip bothered. Trip turned back to John. "That guy in the suit is with the FBI brass in Washington. I have a feeling we're about to meet with at least them, if not the President as well.

"I'm probably not his favorite person right now, am I?" Asked John

"You think?" Trip replied. The two walked over to the man who had entered the room and followed him out of the Oval Office.

Chapter 86

John and Trip followed the man deep down into the White House. John had always heard that there were rooms underneath the building. Now it seemed he was going to find out firsthand. He was sure they wouldn't be shot and dumped down here somewhere . . . well, he was fairly sure.

They finally entered a room and found themselves face to face with the President of the United States. He shook both Trip's and John's hand and offered both of them a seat. After the President sat, John couldn't take the mounting pressure inside and he just began to blurt things out.

"Mr. President, I would like to apologize to you. This case developed so quickly we never had an opportunity to give you a heads up about what was about to happen. I'm sorry if we have caused you any embarrassment." Trip looked at John like he'd like to strangle him. John shrugged. The President nodded and answered.

"John, Trip, neither of you will receive any reprimand in this case if I have anything to do about it," the President responded. John and Trip were both a little taken aback with that. "I asked you here to see if there was anything else you suspect that was not brought to light during my wife's on-air revelations. It is obvious from what I saw today that I have been duped. I now wonder if I have been duped by just Lis . . .Veronica, or also by Archibald Staples." John gave a low whistle, he hadn't thought about that angle yet. John looked at Trip and Trip gestured for him to take lead.

"Sir." John wasn't quite sure what to say; this was the President after all. He decided to talk to him man to man. "Sir, I have no proof about Archibald Staples." The President looked relieved and began to relax in his chair.

"However," the President stopped his relaxing. "I believe Archibald Staples is as dirty as the day is long." Trip looked up at the ceiling and blew air out of his mouth. Trip prayed internally that he would still have his job when this was all over.

"Do you think a fourteen year old child could orchestrate all of those parents being run out of town so easily or the payoff to Mrs. George?" John asked. The President shook his head. He was hearing all of the doubts that he already had himself. "I have not yet begun to dig into this man, but I think there is quite a bit there."

"I think you leave me no choice then, John," said the President. John was suddenly seeing bad mob movies run through his head. He was going to end up buried under the White House! "I will have to divorce my wife, which I would anyway. This has nothing to do with politics; she's just not who I thought she was. I will also have to resign. For all I know Archibald has been using my position for his own gain. There's no telling what Lisa was doing that I wasn't aware of. Even if neither of them did anything, there is too much suspicion for the American people to trust me, and the one thing we cannot have is the people of this country believing that their President is in the pocket of a wealthy businessman, and there being some evidence supporting that." John was impressed.

"Sir, I don't get into politics much, regardless of what some may think," said John. The President smiled catching the obvious reference to John being tied to Senator Cosby. "But what I do know is honor, and what you are getting ready to do sounds like an honorable, but more importantly, the right thing to do." John stood up and offered the President his hand. The President stood up and shook John's hand. "As far as I'm concerned, sir, this talk never happened if that is what you want."

The President buttoned his coat and straightened himself. "I would appreciate that John. I would also appreciate if you would turn over every rock and dig in every hole Lisa and her father had any dealings with. Those two deserve whatever you can find." John smiled and so did the President.

"Sir, you'd better believe they have both made my list." Trip raised his eyebrows.

"How are you going to do that, John? You're just a PI?" Trip asked smugly. Both of them were shocked when the man from the Washington bureau, they had both forgotten was in the room, answered.

"If John wants back in, then there will be no resistance from us," he said. John decided to double down and go for broke.

"And Jessica and Chet?" John asked. Trip groaned inwardly.

The man from the bureau smiled. "John, they are safe. I'm not for sure that you're safe from Arthur Moore."

"There's a shock," said John sarcastically. That brought a chuckle from the man from the bureau which surprised everyone in the room. John and Trip started out of the White House. When they exited John heard Trip chuckle behind him. There, waiting for John, was Bruce.

Chapter 87

Bruce did a slow clap as he walked up to John. Trip ignored the two and walked past them. Trip didn't know if he could take any more excitement today, and he was sure he didn't want to see this exchange.

"John I have to give it to you," Bruce said. "Three years out of the game, and you pull this one off? That is just impressive. Dude, you have got serious skills."

John was a little taken aback. He wasn't sure what game Bruce was playing but John knew he needed to proceed very cautiously.

"Thank you, Bruce. I appreciate that. How did you get here?"

"Oh, a bunch of us jumped in a plane in New York and flew down. The bureau loaned us cars to get down here to the White House to help out if needed. Obviously we weren't. Good job, sir, good job."

John offered out his hand and Bruce shook it. John released Bruce's hand, and was quickly herded off by other agents to begin to answer questions for the reports that had to be filed. Bruce stood and watched John leave. Bruce looked back at the White House. Bruce chuckled and shook his head. Bruce's phone rang. It was a blocked number.

"Bruce Cosby," he answered.

"Mr. Cosby," said the voice on the other end. "I could use your help on a matter; I believe it could make someone's FBI career. If you're interested simply show up at the address I'm going to text you. I will include the time of the meet in the text as well. If not, please disregard this phone call like it never happened." The phone call ended.

"Oh, Archibald," said Bruce quietly to himself. "I have heard your voice too many times over the years not to recognize it. I'll gladly meet you and your cronies. There is nothing I would love to hear more than what plan you have to get your little daughter out of this mess she's in right now. It should be quite enjoyable watching you squirm." Bruce looked around and saw many of the reporters were leaving. "I do wonder where my father got off to. Oh, well, who cares?"

Bruce walked over to the car he was loaned, opened the door and sat in the driver's seat. He suddenly started checking his pockets like he had lost his keys. He finally found what he was looking for in his coat pocket. He pulled out a small cloth bag closed by drawstrings. He opened the bag and looked inside. He smiled as he pulled out the ring. It was a simple gold ring. Inscribed inside, it simply read, "Always yours, John". Bruce replaced the ring in the bag, closed it and made sure it was securely tied. He put the bag back into his pocket and spoke to himself very softly.

"If I had a sister, I wouldn't miss her."

Bruce started the car and headed toward the address that was texted to him by the caller.

New York FBI Offices
Later that Afternoon

Chapter 88

John walked into the FBI building with a smile on his face. He looked around upstairs for Bruce but couldn't find him. He chuckled and walked into Trip's office. Trip looked up and saw him. Trip crossed his arms and leaned back in his chair. John stuck his hands in his pockets and rocked back on his heels.

John spoke, "I guess I haven't made a lot of friends in Washington." Trip choked back a laugh.

"The rumor I got from Washington is the President will announce his resignation this week. The official story will be he is going to help his wife. A few weeks after that will come the sad announcement of their divorce due to irreconcilable differences." John continued to rock back on his heels. Trip dropped his arms from his chest and smiled. "I'm surprised we haven't heard from Bruce's dad. I figure he's one of the ones behind the scenes secretly helping him push Lisa out of the President's life. Senator Cosby will want a photo with you by the way." John began to laugh and clapped his hands together. Trip was grinning broadly. He pulled a folder out of his desk drawer. He handed it John. John took it and looked at the file name. It simply said "Samantha Fowler". John sighed. He started to open it and stopped. John looked out the window and did the hardest thing he had ever done. He handed the file back to Trip. Trip looked dumfounded. "I don't understand, did I do something wrong," asked Trip.

John smiled and replied. "Nope, you didn't do a thing wrong Trip. I'm not ready." Trip looked extremely confused. "I need to tell you something that hardly anyone knows." Trip nodded for him to go ahead. "The night Sam died . . ." John looked away, cleared his throat and continued with tears in his eyes. "The night Sam died, I was heading home. I was going to tell her I was joining AA and leaving the FBI if she wanted me to. I had bought this locket to give to her to apologize with; not that the locket itself was much of an apology with all I had put her through. Anyway, I had been standing a few blocks away trying to think of the right thing to say to her. I couldn't decide. I finally gave up and headed to the apartment . . . well, you know the rest." Trip folded his hands on his desk and looked down; when he looked back up he spoke.

"Did you ever join AA?" Trip asked.

John started to shake his head no, but stopped. "I have gone to many meetings over the past three years. Honestly, for a year I went nearly every day, but . . . I've never spoken or participated. I've just sat and listened to all of these people tell their story. I've never had the courage to tell mine. Trip, part of me feels like if I do, I'm letting go of Sam."

Trip nodded that he understood. When Trip spoke, he did so quietly. "So you left the FBI, but you didn't do the part you promised; mind you it wasn't a promise to yourself, but a promise all the same. You feel like if you do participate, then you will be moving on with your life?" John nodded. "You don't feel that's right, because you think you should have died with her that night?" John nodded again. "You feel like you let Sam down, John?" John nodded, tears streaming down his cheeks.

"Well . . ." Trip picked up the folder he had been working on before John walked in. He opened it up in front on John. "These are your reinstatement papers into the FBI." John was stunned. John knew it was coming, but

230

he was shocked at the speed that it was taking place. Trip continued. "Here's the deal. You do what you have to do, and when you're ready we'll pursue one or both of these files." He was gesturing toward Sam's file and John's reinstatement papers. "But understand this, John Fowler." John was a little stunned by the sudden sternness and fierceness in Trip's voice. "You need to understand that both of us know that you are not done with the FBI, or this case." Trip was holding Sam's folder in his hand to emphasize his point. "You may have a pity party, and cry about the unfairness of it all, but there is a day coming when you will become consumed with only one thought and when that day comes, know that as long as I have one word to say about it . . . The entire FBI will be at your disposal!"

Tears were freely falling down John's cheeks. He didn't even try to speak. He simply reached his hand out and Trip clasped his and spoke. "Go do what you have to do. Take as long as you need. We'll get whoever this is, wherever they are." John nodded and headed out the door. Trip leaned back in his chair after John left. A slow smile crossed his face. He knew he would have his agent back soon, and when he did, they would find out exactly who killed Samantha Fowler.

Chapter 89

John headed down to the foxhole. Chet and Jessica were studying a file on the interactive monitor when he walked in. Chet saw him and waved him over. John walked over and put his arms around both of their shoulders. Jessica raised an eyebrow.

"So you save our jobs, save the first lady from being murdered, cause the president to possibly resign due to his wife's actions over twenty-five years ago, and you think you can just go back to being best buds with us?" Jessica asked.

John smiled, took his arms off of both of their shoulders, and spun Jessica toward him. He caught her in a full bear hug. He whispered in her ear. "Thank you . . . thank you for reminding me of who I am."

Jessica was a shocked. She had never expected such a heartfelt apology from John. Maybe Sam was right. Maybe his outward persona was a defense mechanism. During the exchange, Chet slipped from the room. John let her go and held her shoulders. He spoke. "I'm sorry I held so much against you for so long."

Jessica waved it off. John continued.

"Jessica, I have talked to several people the past couple of days and many of them have told me the same thing. After I went off the deep end after Sam's death, you did all the things I should have done. Jess, you took care of me when the last thing I said to you was how much I hated you. You saw me at my absolute worst in life and did all you could to help me. I don't know how I can ever thank you. Me taking this case and getting certain people off your back at Washington doesn't even start to get us even."

Jessica looked away. John had figured it all out again. John continued. "You kept everyone in the loop . . . well, those that would let you. Let me guess, Arthur didn't think it was right for you to tell him anything. My guess is somehow you got in contact with Sam's mom, Madeline, and told her how the investigation was going."

Jessica shook her head. "How do you do it, John? How do you figure out all of these things no one else can?"

John shrugged. "It's a gift, and sometimes a curse." Jessica punched him in the shoulder. "I'm serious, Jessica. You can't buy me things to surprise me with, or keep secrets because I figure them out. Like the only case you two worked on for the majority of the last three years was Sam's murder case."

Jessica looked down again. "Jess, if you think you failed me because you couldn't solve it, well . . . you're wrong. I failed me and Sam by not solving it then. I don't know if I have the strength to dig back into it now. I don't know if I can survive looking into it. I fear if I reopen that case . . . then I'll go back to drinking, and I'll lose everyone in my life all over again." John reached out and took her hand in his. "I feel like I have a life again and something to look forward to. I don't think I could bear to lose all of that again."

Jessica looked at John. She looked a little nervous and asked him the question she had been dreading. "So . . . what about us?"

John stepped back. The slow grin returned to his face and he spoke.

"I don't know. I don't know about returning to the FBI yet." He looked at Jessica's face, but he saw he hadn't answered the question she had really been asking. "As for what else may be implied by that question, let me say this. I'm not ready for anything today. I said earlier we have a relationship, and I meant that. I just don't know how far I'm ready to take it right now. I honestly mean this when I say, it's not you; it's me." Jessica raised an eyebrow. "Jess . . . I have something I have to take care of first. A promise

I made to Sam." Jessica looked down. When she looked back at John her eyes were sparkling.

"John, I have no idea if there is an us. I don't know if there could be, but if you don't do something soon, there never will be."

John nodded. "I have to go do something. I have to take care of something tonight, and it would mean a lot to me if you were there. If there is to be an us, I have to take care of this first." John handed her a card and Jessica looked at it. When she looked back up at John there were tears in her eyes and she was nodding. He continued. "Meet me there at 8:00 tonight if you can. If not, I'll talk to you tomorrow." John stepped up to Jessica and kissed her on the cheek. John turned and left. After he left the room, Jessica continued to rub her cheek where John had kissed it. She smiled, and promised herself she would meet him tonight.

Chapter 90

As John walked up to the podium he thought about the last four years. He thought of Sam and for the first time in a long time, tears didn't well up in his eyes as he thought about her, but instead a smile crossed his face. He also thought of Jessica, and to his surprise he didn't feel like he was cheating on Sam when he thought of Jess. That caught him a little off guard. John chuckled to himself. He wasn't sure what the future was going to hold, but he had to do this if there ever was to be a future for them.

"Sam," John thought to himself. "I didn't die that day. I have to move on with my life and the only way to do it is to do the things I promised you I would. I'm sorry you are gone, but I'm not and I have to do this for me to have a life; to honor yours." He swore he felt her giving him an encouraging push.

He took a deep breath. He stepped up to the podium and looked around all the men and women sitting. Jessica sat in the front row. She smiled encouragingly. He thought to himself privately, "Sam, this is for you." He looked back toward Jessica expecting to see Sam. Sam wasn't there, only Jessica. John spoke to the audience that had gathered.

"Hello . . . my name is John Fowler . . . and I'm an alcoholic."

Arthur Moore
Sam's Parents House, Virginia

Chapter 91

Arthur Moore, Sam's father, was watching the news recap. He stared at John's picture on TV. Anger and hatred welled up inside. He looked away from the TV and studied the trust document in his hand again. Madeline, Arthur's wife, joined him in the room. She saw the program that he was watching and shook her head.

"Arthur, I wish you would let this go, but if you can't, then make the phone call. I want you to get closure."

Arthur looked at his wife. "Maddie, it's not fair! That man chews us out at our own daughter's funeral and then goes and hides from the world for over three years? Then, when he finally decides to do something, it is to save the life of that Staples girl? Don't get me wrong, I'm sorry for what she did to that family years ago, but you and I both know Archibald will get her out of this mess!" Arthur stood up and began to walk around the room while Madeline watched him from the couch. Arthur continued.

"It's not right, Maddie! John doesn't get to walk away and not do something about Sam! He doesn't!" Madeline stood up and walked over to her husband. She put her arms on his shoulders from behind, attempting to comfort him.

"Arthur," she said. She turned him around to face her. "Arthur the poor boy's been grieving all of these years." Arthur walked away, tears brimming in his face.

"And I haven't?!" Arthur exclaimed. Maddie shook her head.

"Then, Arthur, make the phone call," Maddie said.

Arthur Moore picked up the phone and made the phone call that would change John Fowler's life forever.

The Next Morning
John's PI Office

Chapter 92

John was whistling as he walked. He had checked his messages for the PI Office earlier from his home. Apparently his business phone had been ringing off the hook the night before and all that morning with the notoriety he had received from saving the first lady's life . . . and with the apparent resignation of the president. He had listened to a few of the calls. Most were more of the same type of cases he'd dealt with in the past. He really didn't want to go back to those divorce and cheating spouse cases, not after the FBI case he had just completed. He shuddered involuntarily at some of the old PI cases that entered his thoughts.

John had never more felt alive. He wasn't for sure how long this feeling would last, but for right now, it was enough. He hadn't thought twice about walking away from Sam's case file. He was seriously thinking over Trip's offer of a return to the FBI. He didn't know what he would do. Chet had all but begged John to return, and Jessica had acted indifferent about his return. Jessica said they could still have a relationship and John not be a part of the FBI.

John didn't know how he would feel about that. He could see them talking at dinner or some other place where they were together about what they did that day. John didn't think he could stand listening to Jessica tell him about some exciting case and then have to tell her about stalking out two very unattractive people to take pictures of them doing unspeakable things to each other for their spouses. The earlier PI cases reentered his thoughts, and John shivered again at the mental image.

John realized what he had just thought about; having a date with Jessica. Things had changed so much for him in the past couple of weeks. Heck, things had changed so much in the past two days! After the AA meeting last night he and Jessica had talked until two in the morning at the coffee shop about Sam. Well that wasn't true. They talked about Sam for a little while and then they talked about the two of them. It felt great! John felt like he finally had a life!

John knew Sam would want him to move on, but John wasn't sure he could have a relationship with Jessica and remain sane. Jessica knew all of John's faults. Jessica had literally seen him at the worst place he had ever been in his life, and she still wanted to be with him. That was some pretty heavy stuff, and John wasn't completely sure how he felt about it all. John shook his head and tried to stop thinking about his love life . . . or lack thereof. That was another thought for another day. John turned the corner, and stopped dead in his tracks. Apparently he was wrong, that was a thought for right now. John chuckled and waved to Jessica who was waiting in front of his building. She looked at her watch as he walked up.

"I don't know, John. I don't think you can punch a time clock on time in the FBI any longer," she said.

"How do you do it?" John asked. Jessica raised her eyebrows. "How do you stay up past 2:00 am and still look so wonderful?"

"Flattery will get you nowhere with me, Mr. Fowler, but you're welcome to continue to try," Jessica said as she put her arms around John's neck. John's heart began to hammer in his chest. He knew Jessica was enjoying this. She was trying to mess with him, and she was doing an excellent job! To be totally honest John was enjoying being messed with! Jessica leaned in very close to his ear and whispered.

"John, I should have said this last night, but I couldn't. Let me say what I need to say now." John nodded, Jessica smiled coyly and continued. "John, I need you. I don't think I can make it without you. I'm lost without you John. I have never told a soul that before. John, please stay."

John's heart was about to jackhammer out of his chest. Jessica could feel it beating against her. She leaned back and took a look at him.

"John . . . are you okay?" John nodded and summoned the strength to speak.

"Jess . . . are you talking about the FBI?" Jessica smiled and touched her finger to his nose. She turned and walked away. Over her shoulder, she answered.

"John, what else would I be talking about? See you later."

John took a few minutes to compose himself. He smiled and began to whistle again as he headed up the building stairs to his office. John's whistle died on his lips as he noticed a figure through the window of his office.

John opened the door and walked in. A very well dressed man was sitting on his couch. The man smiled.

"John, John Fowler?"

Something in John's mind screamed not to answer and to walk out the door, but instead John answered, "Yes." The man smiled and handed John a folded piece of paper.

"John Fowler, you've been served."

John sighed. He knew deep down what was coming before the man had served him. He had to get back on his game. That was the problem with this happy feeling; he missed the little things that he normally would have noticed. John laughed. Apparently there had to be a certain balance between happiness and sadness for him to be most effective. John sat down and looked at the summons. He decided to go ahead and open it and get everything over it. His mouth dropped as he read the document. His in-laws were suing him in civil court! Not only that, they were suing him for the death of Sam. His in-laws were asking for the trust that Sam's grandparents had left to Sam and him to be turned over to them. John let the paper fall to his desk. John stood up and looked out his window trying to decide what to do. His cell phone began to ring. He looked down and saw the title, "Mommy." John answered, thinking Chet had been served as well.

"Chet, did they serve you too?"

"John, I don't know what you're talking about, but this is huge. Bruce's father has been kidnapped!"

"What? When?"

"We're not for sure; it was just reported about an hour ago . . . John, Bruce is asking for your help."

John looked out the window as the slow smile crossed his face. While he felt sorry for United States senator Jeremiah Cosby, the fact Bruce had to break down and ask for his help made John's day.

Chet was still talking. "John! John! Are you there?"

"I'm here, Chet. I'll be there in twenty minutes."

The End . . . For Now.

www.ingramcontent.com/pod-product-compliance
Lightning Source LLC
Chambersburg PA
CBHW071309250626
47159CB00004B/1360